KT-165-010

CAERDYDD
CARDIFF

ACC. No: 07001011

THE
DOLDRUMS

Written and illustrated by

NICHOLAS GANNON

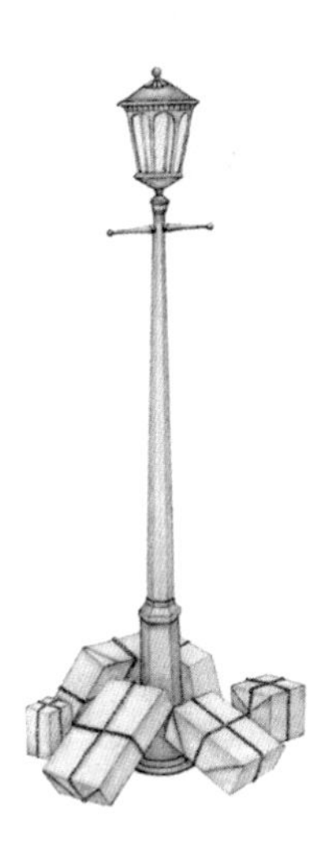

HarperCollins *Children's Books*

First published in the USA by HarperCollins *Publishers* Inc. in 2015
First published in Great Britain by HarperCollins *Children's Books* in 2015
HarperCollins *Children's Books* is a division of HarperCollins *Publishers* Ltd,
HarperCollins Publishers
1 London Bridge Street
London SE1 9GF
The HarperCollins *Children's Books* website address is
www.harpercollins.co.uk

1

ISBN 978-0-00-814939-0

Printed in China

To my mother,

Cathleen Gannon

✦ Table of Contents ✦

✦ Great White Nothingness ✦

Out of the thousands of children born every single day, at least one of them will turn out to be a dreamer. And on May the fifth, in room 37E of the maternity ward at Rosewood Hospital, that one child was Archer Benjamin Helmsley. Yes, there was simply no mistaking it. The doctors saw it, the nurses saw it, and much to her chagrin, his mother saw it. Even a pigeon that wandered into the viewing room station saw it.

The young Archer B. Helmsley lay quietly in the maternity ward, staring at the ceiling. He didn't know it was a ceiling. He didn't know what anything was. But Archer lay there all the same, gazing up into that great white nothingness, when all at once, two heads sprouted from nowhere.

"Why hello there," said one of the heads. "You *must* be Archer."

"Yes," agreed the second head. "He truly *must* be Archer."

Whether he must be Archer or not, Archer was Archer, but Archer himself didn't know that yet.

"Do you know who we are?" asked the first head.

"How could he?" said the second. "He's only forty-eight hours old."

The first head agreed. "In that case, I believe introductions are in order. I'm your Grandpa Helmsley and this—*this* is your Grandma Helmsley."

Archer didn't respond because Archer couldn't respond. There's really not much you can do when you're only forty-eight hours old. But the two heads went on and on about this and that, and Archer looked from one to the other, not understanding a single word. Then a third head sprouted from nowhere and just as quickly, all three disappeared, leaving Archer to stare at the ceiling.

• Helmsleys of 375 Willow Street •

Three days later, Archer was released from Rosewood Hospital and carried to a tall, skinny house on a crooked narrow street in a quiet neighborhood of a not-so-quiet city.

Archer was too little to notice that all of the houses on Willow Street were tall and skinny and stacked one next to the other, like a row of tin soldiers. Archer was also too little to know that his house, number 375, was frequently mistaken for a museum. You see, Archer's house belonged to Archer's grandparents, the renowned explorers and naturalists Ralph and Rachel Helmsley.

HELMSLEY HOUSE

375 WILLOW STREET

• Wandering & Wondering •

Some parents may wonder, *How do we know we have the right one?* after bringing their child home from the hospital. If Mr. and Mrs. Helmsley had such thoughts of their own, they were quickly extinguished. From the very beginning, Archer showed all the signs of being a Helmsley.

DOLDRUMS PRESS

During his early years, Archer had a fairly perfect life. Fortunately, his fairly perfect life didn't last very long. Why is that fortunate?

7
5

We all know perfect boys and perfect girls. They live in perfect houses owned by perfect parents. They dress perfectly and walk perfectly and live their lives in the most perfectly perfect way. It's perfectly terrible. They're perfectly dull. So it's fortunate this story is about no such child.

This is the story of Archer Benjamin Helmsley.

37

THE
DOLDRUMS

✦ PART ONE ✦

ARCHER B. HELMSLEY

CHAPTER ONE

✦ Helmsley House ✦

Archer didn't have a dog or cat like many children do, but he did have an ostrich, a badger, and a giraffe. Helmsley House was filled with creatures, on all four floors and in all of the rooms. They lined the narrow staircases and still narrower halls. They were all stuffed with fluff and couldn't do a thing, but that didn't bother Archer. And because he had no brothers or sisters to speak to, Archer spoke to the animals.

"Good morning, badger," Archer said on his way to the kitchen. "How's the weather?"

"I'm sorry to say the rainy autumn continues," the badger replied. "This moisture does a terrible number on the fur. Just look at this poof."

Archer gave the badger a pat on the head.

"I never would have noticed," he lied. (The badger's fur

always looked a frightful mess when the humidity was high.)

Mrs. Helmsley poked her head from the kitchen door.

"Who are you speaking to?" she asked.

"*Oh*—no one," said Archer. "Just myself."

He stepped beneath his mother's frown and into the kitchen.

After eating his breakfast of tea with milk and toast with jam, Archer began exploring. He wandered down the first-floor hallway and into the conservatory, a glass room filled with glass cases that stuck out into the back garden, and pressed his face against one that was filled with bizarre jungle insects.

It's good these are dead, he thought. One, he was certain, would turn his head purple if it latched onto his toe. Another, he assumed, would dig its way under his skin and decide to start a family deep inside. *Very good indeed.*

Along the walls were more glass cases holding row after row of neatly aligned butterflies. Archer noted these were not of the variety one might take an interest in and chase after. On the contrary, it appeared as though these might take an interest in and chase after you.

"Best to avoid these butterflies," he said to the giraffe.

"A wise choice, my dear," the giraffe replied. "I shudder every time I look at them."

"Do you think we should even call them butterflies?" he asked.

"Perhaps a name like *shudderflies* would be more accurate," said the giraffe.

Archer grinned. "Yes. These are definitely shudderflies."

He turned to leave, but nearly hit the ceiling when he discovered his mother standing behind him. Her hands were holding her hips in place.

"Who are you speaking to?" she insisted.

"*Oh*—no one," he replied. "Just myself."

Archer slipped beneath her furrowed brow and continued on his way.

• Glockenspiel & Scuttlebutt •

Archer's mother, Helena E. Helmsley, hosted frequent dinner parties at Helmsley House. The guests of these events were always eager to see the home that belonged to the renowned explorers. Archer, on the other hand, was never excited to see the guests.

"It's going to be a big one tonight," he said, consoling the ostrich with a pat on the back.

"Don't touch me," snapped the ostrich. "I told you not to come near me with those filthy hands."

Archer apologized and slowly backed away. (The ostrich was like that sometimes.)

It's often the case that adults look at children as if they

were nothing more than bizarre museum exhibits. For a boy like Archer, in a house like his, this treatment was worse. Much worse. So on these nights he tried his best, often with little success, to escape upstairs.

"Archer," said Mrs. Helmsley, just as he put his foot on the stair. "I would like to introduce you to Mr. Glockenspiel. He owns an award-winning ballpoint pen factory in Germany."

Archer turned and approached this well-whiskered man.

"Good evening, Mr. Glob of Seal," he said.

Mr. Glockenspiel frowned. Mr. Helmsley tried his best not to laugh. Mrs. Helmsley found the task much simpler.

"It's *Glockenspiel*," she insisted. "Glock—en—spiel."

"That is correct," huffed the Glob of Seal.

Archer was glad this man's name was not Glob of Seal. You wouldn't go very far with a name like that.

"I'm sorry, Mr. Gawk and Squeal," he said.

Mr. Helmsley nearly burst. Mrs. Helmsley grabbed Archer's arm. She ushered him away from the Glob of Seal and assigned him the task of carrying a tray of cucumbers around to the guests.

"Just smile and nod," she said, her hazel eyes looking terribly grave. "There's no need to say another word tonight."

While making his cucumber rounds, Archer spotted a scraggly looking gentleman sneaking down the halls as though he knew them well. Archer was curious and followed and watched as the man stumbled into an empty room. Archer poked his head through the door, but nearly shouted and dropped the cucumbers when he discovered the man staring straight back at him. The man nodded for Archer to enter, then eased himself into an armchair.

Archer stood silently before the stranger, thinking he looked most out of place at his mother's dinner party. And though this man was old, his pale green eyes sparkled with life.

"You must be Archer Helmsley," he said with a warm smile. "The wonderful grandson to Ralph and Rachel Helmsley. And you come bearing gifts, I see."

Archer lifted the tray. "Would you like a cucumber?" he asked.

"Never cared for them much," the man admitted, and twisted his head around the room while keeping his eyes on Archer. "Your grandparents have a lovely house. What do you think of them?"

Archer shrugged. "I've never met them," he replied.

The man nodded. "I can't say I'm surprised, but I'm sure you will soon enough." He then lowered his voice, despite no one else's being in the room. "Between you and me, they wouldn't be terribly thrilled about all these gatherings riddled with scuttlebutt filling the great halls of Helmsley House."

Archer wasn't sure what *scuttlebutt* meant, but it made him smile. And he was glad to hear his grandparents weren't fond of dinner parties either.

"There's a fascinating world out there, Archer Helmsley," the man continued. "But you'd never know that looking at these people." He glanced at his watch. "Now I'm sorry to say I must be going. Mind giving me a shoulder?"

Archer lowered the tray.

"We'd best go as quickly as possible," the man said, standing up and taking hold of Archer's shoulder. "We want to avoid your—" he stopped.

Archer stared up at him. "Avoid who?" he asked.

The man smiled and shook his head. "Oh, no one," he replied. "We just don't want to get stuck in an *undesirable* conversation."

Archer agreed. There were plenty of those on such nights. But he knew his house well and led the man on a roundabout way, through empty halls and down the stairs, till they arrived at the door without anyone being the wiser.

The man stood on the front steps, silhouetted in a silver streak by the streetlamps, and gazed down at him.

"Do they always dress you up like a Christmas tree?" he asked.

Archer's green velvet suit and red dotted bow tie did make him look rather festive. Mrs. Helmsley said he looked like a gentleman, but Archer agreed with this man. He looked like a Christmas tree.

The man placed a firm hand on Archer's shoulder and said, "Always remember you're a Helmsley, Archer. And being a Helmsley means something."

He turned to leave, but Archer stopped him with a question.

"How do you know my grandparents?" he asked.

"That's a long story," the man replied, without turning around. "Remind me to tell you the next time we meet."

Archer watched the man hobble down the sidewalk, a little afraid he might stumble into oncoming traffic, until a hand reached out and shut the door.

"Who was that?" Mrs. Helmsley asked.

"I don't know," said Archer. "But he knows Grandma and Grandpa."

Archer wished he were as lucky as that man. He'd never met his grandparents. They'd been traveling the world ever since he was born. To Archer, Ralph and Rachel Helmsley were a mystery wrapped in a secret—a secret he very much wanted to know. But his mother always changed the subject whenever their names were mentioned.

"Where's your tray?" she asked.

Archer sighed and retrieved the tray, to continue with his cucumber rounds. "*You're a Helmsley . . . and being a Helmsley means something.*" Archer wasn't sure what that meant, but he was fairly certain it had nothing to do with cucumbers. Still, he weaved his way through the crowded rooms and was about to attempt a second escape when the porcupine on the radiator asked if it might try one.

"Yes," said Archer. "But not in front of these people."

He took the creature into the empty dining room.

"Those taste awful," said the porcupine.

Archer tried one and agreed. He left the prickly fellow on a chair and went to the kitchen to find something better. While he was away, the guests entered the dining room to take their seats. Mr. Glockenspiel failed to notice that his seat was already occupied and hastily plopped his derriere right atop the porcupine. Archer returned from the kitchen but stopped in the doorway, watching as the guests gawked and Mr. Glockenspiel squealed. His father alone seemed to enjoy the scene.

"It was him!" shouted the Glob of Seal, rubbing his rear and pointing his chubby finger at Archer.

Mrs. Helmsley spun around in her chair and looked as though she was the one who'd just sat atop the porcupine.

"Did you do this?" she demanded.

Archer didn't know what to say, so he didn't say anything.

It was no secret to him that little he did pleased his mother. And he knew she wasn't as fond of the house as he was. But Mrs. Helmsley wasn't a Helmsley by blood, and that's often how it goes.

Things were different with his father.

• Gaudy Little Fellow •

Archer's father, Richard B. Helmsley, was a lawyer. Archer didn't know much about lawyers, and to be honest, he wasn't interested. What did interest him were the secret trips he and his father took. These began when Archer was seven years old, and they had to be done in secret because his mother wouldn't like the idea.

"Psst," Mr. Helmsley had whispered one day.

"Hello!" blurted Archer.

"Shhh," shushed his father.

"Why are we whispering," whispered Archer.

"No time to explain. Follow me."

Archer followed his father out the front door and down the sidewalk.

"Where are we going?" he asked.

Mr. Helmsley had led him to Rosewood Park, which was more like a dark and unruly forest. Its winding walkways quickly vanished, but straight ahead, rising high above the thick canopy and glowing a brilliant orange, loomed the Rosewood Museum towers. Archer thought the museum was ancient, built with flourishes of terra-cotta and capped with a moldy green roof. The front gardens were in need of some attention, but he liked the weathered majesty of it all.

Once inside, he followed his father down countless corridors filled with countless oddities and listened to stories of how his father almost became the greatest explorer of countless places.

"And then I almost became the world's greatest explorer of Egypt," said Mr. Helmsley as they approached a sarcophagus belonging to the late Pharaoh Tappenkuse.

Archer admired his father and liked his stories, but knew he was a lawyer.

"Why didn't you actually do it," he asked.

Mr. Helmsley stuck his hands into his blazer pockets. It was a simple question, but adults often complicate simplicity. And as with his mother when he asked about his grandparents, Mr. Helmsley always changed the subject when Archer asked this.

"Did you know this gaudy little fellow was one of the youngest pharaohs to ever rule Egypt?" he said, discreetly reading from a museum guide. "Tappy here was only thirteen years old when he became king."

After glancing over Tappy, Archer decided it was for the best there weren't many thirteen-year-old kings. "He looks depressed."

"I think that's just the eyeliner," said Mr. Helmsley.

He licked a finger and reached for the sarcophagus.

"No touching," said a security guard.

"Sorry," said Mr. Helmsley.

"Did he want to become king?" asked Archer.

His father wasn't sure. "He only ruled for two years before he died."

Archer was taken aback. "Well, I don't think he wanted to become king then," he said, and stepped away from Tappenkuse.

Archer listened to a few more stories about his father's almost adventures and then followed him to the exit and down the sidewalk home. He was thinking about his grandparents as they walked.

"What are they like in person and why are they never home?" he asked. "When am I going to meet them?"

"You met them when you were little," Mr. Helmsley said.

Archer doubted this. He had no memory of it.

As they climbed the steps back to Helmsley House, Archer spotted a package leaning against the door. It was wrapped in brown paper and tied with red string and addressed to him. Archer quickly scooped it up.

"What's that?" Mr. Helmsley asked.

"What's what?" said Archer, hiding it behind his back. "It's nothing."

"It doesn't look like nothing."

At that moment, their neighbor Mr. Glub stepped out of his house and called to Mr. Helmsley. "Haven't seen you in a while!"

Mr. Helmsley waved and went back down the steps to speak with him. Archer slipped inside and up to his room.

• Eye to Glass Eye •

Archer stepped into his closet, turned on the light, and pushed aside his clothes hangers to reveal an entire bookshelf brimming with packages. All of these were from his grandparents and he kept them a secret because his grandfather suggested it in a letter—but also because he liked having a secret to keep. He sat down on the floor, pulled the red string, and tore back the paper.

ARCHER B. HELMSLEY
375 WILLOW STREET

15TH OF OCTOBER

ARCHER,

THIS IS A LITTLE ODD BUT WE THOUGHT YOU MIGHT LIKE IT. A SHIP'S CAPTAIN GAVE IT TO US. HE WAS THE ONLY ONE WHO KNEW HOW TO GET US TO AN ISLAND MOUNTAIN THE LOCALS REFERRED TO AS "DEATH MOUNTAIN."

IT WAS A TINY MOUNTAIN REALLY. SHOT STRAIGHT UP OUT OF THE WATER AND WAS SPOTTED WITH TREES. IT WAS MORE BEAUTIFUL THAN ITS NAME MADE YOU THINK.

ENCLOSED IS A GLASS EYE. HIS GLASS EYE. HE ONLY HAD ONE EYE. THE CAPTAIN DID. BUT THAT DIDN'T BOTHER HIM. HE GAVE IT TO US ON THE RETURN SO WE WOULDN'T FORGET SEEING THE MOUNTAIN.

YOURS TRULY,

Ralph and Rachel Helmsley

Archer looked at the glass eye. The glass eye looked back at Archer. He picked it up and held it to his own, thinking he might be able to see the mountain, but all he saw was the back of a glass eye.

Archer longed to meet his grandparents. Judging from their letters and house, they must be magnificent people. But when would they return? Soon, he hoped. He was growing bored with his quiet life on Willow Street. More than anything, he wanted to embark on an expedition with them. An adventure—an unusual and strange adventure—like being carried by a pelican to the edge of the world with a pocket full of pebbles, where he could skip his stones from that great height and watch as they careened into darkness.

Mrs. Helmsley had different ideas. Whenever the question was raised of what Archer wished to be, she would answer before he could.

"He wants to be a respectable lawyer like his father," she would say.

Archer used to argue this, but realized it wasn't worth it. He could never win an argument with his mother. And for this, he didn't have to. All he had to do was wait for his grandparents to return. They would set things straight.

• News Is Bad News •

On the morning of his ninth birthday, Archer opened the front door hoping to discover a new package bearing his name, but instead, discovered a newspaper bearing the names of his grandparents.

May 5th $1.50

The Doldrums Press

EXPLORERS VANISH IN ARCTIC WATERS

The renowned explorers Ralph and Rachel Helmsley embarked on an expedition to Antarctica with the intention of documenting the relational habits of penguins. During their voyage south, Ralph spotted an iceberg hosting two separate colonies of penguin.

"We must get closer," he said. "I'm getting on that iceberg."

The captain directed the ship as close as was safe and the deck crew lowered a dinghy into the water. Ralph and Rachel steered the dinghy toward that mighty chunk of ice and climbed on top.

During their investigation atop the iceberg, the skies clouded overhead and snow began falling. Ralph Helmsley said they would return to the ship in one hour, but after two, there was still no sign of them.

The captain watched a quiet haze descend over the iceberg. He blew the horn a number of times, hoping to guide them back, but the Helmsleys did not return. The captain sounded the alarm.

As quickly as was possible, crew members assembled into a search party. They attached a security line to the ship and lowered a second dinghy into the water.

Their search was long. The iceberg was massive. They did not find Helmsleys. All they found was a penguin and Ralph Helmsley's cap.

After returning to the ship, the captain cut the engines.

"All eyes on deck," he shouted.

The crew stood at the railing and scanned the hazy silhouette of the iceberg in silence, hoping to see or hear something, but all they heard were the waves below.

The weather worsened. The iceberg vanished. The crew gave up.

Out of options, the captain started the engines and the Helmsleys were left stranded. While there is no proof to suggest they are dead, it doesn't look good.

—Aubrey Glub
Editor-in-Chief

Archer stood in quiet disbelief, barefoot on the doorstep.

Did penguins eat my grandparents? He wondered. *Is that even possible?*

He slammed the door and ran to the kitchen.

"Grandma and Grandpa are stuck on an iceberg!" he shouted.

Mr. Helmsley sipped his coffee. Mrs. Helmsley poked her egg.

"An *iceberg*!" he repeated.

Mr. and Mrs. Helmsley already knew what had happened. The day before, a letter had been delivered to Helmsley & Durbish:

Richard Helmsley,

I regret to inform you that Ralph and Rachel have vanished at sea atop an iceberg—an event that has shaken almost everyone at the Society. We hope for the best and will keep you informed of any developments.

Sad Regards,
Herbert P. Birthwhistle
~~*Ralph B. Helmsley*~~
The Society President

But they had mentioned nothing of this to Archer.

Within the hour of the newspaper's hitting the doorstep, reporters swooped in from all directions to that tall, skinny house on Willow Street. They held cameras and notepads and shouted questions at Mr. and Mrs. Helmsley, who stood in the doorway. Archer watched the chaos from the roof.

It was the worst birthday Archer could remember. He stared blankly at his vanilla cake (which bore an unfortunate resemblance to an iceberg) while listening to his parents argue in the hallway.

"Don't pretend you don't know who he takes after," his mother said.

"You're overreacting," his father replied.

"It's for his own good."

Archer didn't know what that was about, but he would find out soon enough. All at once, the secret trips with his father came to an abrupt end, he received no more packages tied with red string, and things only got worse from there. There was no further news on Ralph and Rachel Helmsley. With time, the reporters lost interest in the story and a quiet haze settled over Archer's tall, skinny house on crooked, narrow Willow Street.

CHAPTER TWO

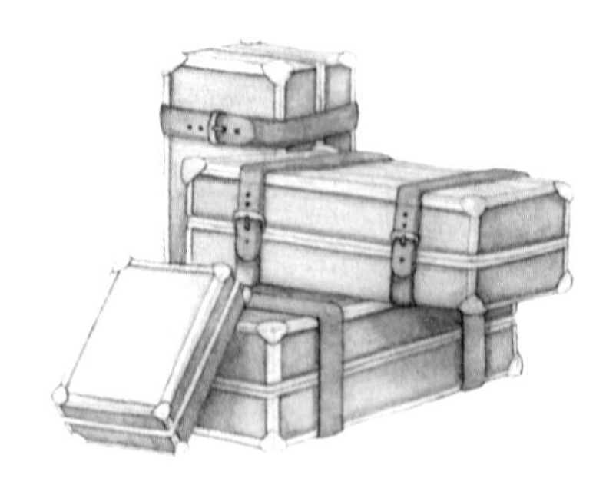

• Mind Your Tongue •

Two years had passed since the iceberg incident, and Archer was now eleven years old. Mr. Helmsley spent most of his time in his study and at the office, and Mrs. Helmsley busied herself about the house. It was a Saturday. But Archer wasn't outside. Aside from school, he never was. This was his mother's decision.

"What happened to your grandparents?" she asked on a regular basis.

"An iceberg," mumbled Archer.

"You must speak up," she replied. "Enunciate."

"An iceberg," said Archer. "They floated out to sea atop an iceberg."

"That's right. They floated out to sea atop an iceberg. And do *you* want to float out to sea atop an iceberg?"

This was not the sort of question that could go either way. This question had a right answer and a wrong answer.

"But there are no icebergs in Rosewood," said Archer.

That didn't matter. If it wasn't an iceberg, it would be something else. After eleven years, Mrs. Helmsley was well aware of Archer's *tendencies*, as she so often put it. Archer was like his grandparents. And that wouldn't do. Mrs. Helmsley had no desire to see Archer drift out to sea atop an iceberg.

"And I don't want to read another newspaper article aimed at embarrassing us."

So when Archer wasn't at school, he spent most of his time assisting his mother with tedious tasks around the house such as dusting the animals (which he still spoke to when she wasn't around), polishing the wood floors, and today, licking a mountain of envelopes and stamps for a neighborhood mailer.

Willow Street Flower Festival

The spring blossoms were stunning and I look forward to seeing what everyone is cooking up for the summer festival: Saturday, July 10th. And save the date for the autumn festival: Saturday, September 27th.

By the time he used all of the stamps, Archer had a paper cut on his tongue and his mouth was rife with glue.

"That's all there is," he said, and stood up to leave.

"Hold it," his mother replied.

A large pile of unstamped envelopes sat next to her. She grabbed her purse and went to buy more stamps. Archer groaned and plunked his head to the table. This was not how things were supposed to be in Helmsley House. Helmsley House was a shrine to exploration and adventure. Not a place to spend your days licking stamps.

Archer had always thought his grandparents would return and whisk him off to incredible places. Instead, they whisked themselves onto an iceberg and Archer was left alone. He continued thumping his head up and down. The doorbell rang. Archer paused, thinking he'd knocked himself silly, but there followed a second ring. He poked his head into the hall.

"Don't answer it," said the badger. The fox agreed. But Archer went to the door.

• Scarlet Trunks •

Not only was someone ringing, but they were also jostling the doorknob up and down. Archer was too short to reach the peephole, so he went to the window and pressed his face to the glass. The front steps were cluttered with trunks that hid whomever they belonged to.

It's them! he thought, dashing back to the door.

Archer threw it open, but the man who stood before him was not his grandfather. This man was tall and slender and wore a dingy jumpsuit stained with grease and grime and smelling of gasoline. He had a kind face and a gentle eye, but only one. An eye patch covered the other. Archer swallowed hard.

He's here for the glass eye! Archer thought.

"So this is the Helmsley House," said the Eye Patch, peering over Archer's head and around the foyer. "I've heard it was lovely, but this is the first I've seen it with my own eye!" He directed that eye at Archer. "Are you Archer?" he asked.

Archer went prickly and nodded carefully. *He knows my name?*

The Eye Patch must have sensed his unease because he quickly stood to the side and pointed at the trunks.

"I'm only here to deliver these," he said. "They belonged to Ralph and Rachel—were at the Society in Barrow's Bay for nearly two years. Not sure why no one brought them before."

The trunks were scarlet, well-worn, and beautiful.

"These belonged to them?" Archer asked.

The Eye Patch nodded. "Mind if I bring them inside?"

Archer helped the man lug the trunks into the foyer. There were five in total, and once they were all inside, the Eye Patch returned to the front steps.

"Those trunks won't be in here for long," he said with a somber look in his eye. "I know what everyone thinks, but I put my bets on your grandparents being alive."

Archer wanted to believe that. "It's been two years," he said.

"That's true," the Eye Patch admitted. "But Ralph and Rachel have seen worse." He glanced over his shoulder. "Now I'd best be running. A few of your neighbors looked like they might call the police—don't think they see many greasy eye patches roaming Willow Street these days."

Archer would have smiled, but he was too busy wondering who this man was. Before he could ask, the Eye Patch tapped a finger to his forehead and disappeared down the sidewalk.

Archer shut the door and knelt before a scarlet trunk, grateful his mother wasn't home. She wouldn't have let these into the house. But he had to be quick. She was only getting stamps. He clicked the latch on the trunk, lifted the lid, and all at once he was surrounded with peculiar smells—a bit of seaweed, a whiff of mist, and a faint yet distinguishable hint of swamp.

Inside the trunk were his grandfather's belongings, but just as he began to dig, he stopped. There were footsteps outside. Someone was at the door. *His mother*. Archer slammed the trunk, grabbed the smallest one, and dashed upstairs. As he sprung for his bedroom, a shrill yelp sounded from the foyer. He threw the trunk under his bed and casually returned downstairs.

The trunks were already gone, and in their place stood a dusty and sweaty Mrs. Helmsley who looked at him as if he had a spider crawling on his forehead.

"Have you been upstairs this whole time?" she asked.

Archer nodded. "I was trying to brush the glue off my tongue," he replied. "Why?"

Mrs. Helmsley wiped a dirty hand against her cheek. It made a streak.

"It doesn't matter," she replied. "That's the end of it. Now, into the kitchen—I have more stamps."

Archer couldn't stop guessing what was inside the trunks as he licked his way through a second mountain of stamps. When Mrs. Helmsley released him, he hurried upstairs with three more paper cuts on his tongue.

• Helmsley Golden Age •

Archer sat on his bed across from the small trunk. Inside he found a pair of binoculars, a bundle of old journals, and a tape labeled "audio conversion."

Archer untied the journals and carefully flipped through the pages. They were filled with details of his grandparents' travels, and from the dates he figured they had been around twenty-seven when they wrote them. Archer had leaned back on his bed and was reading a journal when something struck him. He sat up and removed the tape.

"'Audio conversion,'" he mumbled. "But that means—"

He ran from his room with the tape in hand.

At the end of a narrow third-floor hallway was a large room lined with skinny windows on one side and maps on the other. Stretching down the center was a long wooden table littered with more maps and globes. Archer hurried past it to the corner of the room, where a smaller table held a complex audio system. He inserted the tape and sat down.

For all its dials and gauges and knobs, the system had one simple on/off switch. Archer clicked it and hit another, but instead of hearing his grandparents' voices, he heard static and a voice saying, "*Bonjour?*"

Archer grabbed the microphone. "Brochure?" he asked.

"*Oui, bonjour.*"

"Free brochure?"

"*Oui! Bonjour.*"

"Thanks, but I'm not interested in a free brochure."

Archer wasn't sure who this person was or what they were selling, but he didn't care. He flipped a different switch. The tape clicked on and began rolling. Archer leaned forward.

P.B.H.

TAPE START

A LOUD CRASH / A STRANGE SQUAWK / THE POURING OF TEA / AND THEN THE VOICES OF GRANDMA AND GRANDPA HELMSLEY

GRANDPA HELMSLEY: Is it on? That light is blinking at me. Does that mean this thing is recording?

GRANDMA HELMSLEY: I think so. Yes, it must.

GRANDPA HELMSLEY: All right, this is first in a series to convert our journals into audio.

GRANDMA HELMSLEY: Would you like some tea?

GRANDPA HELMSLEY: Yes, very good, thank you. Let's see, I suppose we could begin with—*oh*—careful with your tea! I think I—yes, I just burned my tongue.

GRANDMA HELMSLEY: You'll be fine, dear. We're wasting tape. Here, take this one. Let's begin with Egypt. And before we do, it should be noted that we were much younger in those days.

GRANDPA HELMSLEY: Good idea. Let's start with a bang. *CLEARS THROAT*. After spending hours poring over maps and charting our course, the plane was readied and we set off for Egypt. A defective compass led to a series of wrong turns, but we adjusted our course and continued across the sea.

GRANDMA HELMSLEY: But we wasted much fuel in the process and didn't have enough to complete the journey.

GRANDPA HELMSLEY: As we reached the desert sands, the sun

was beginning to set and the engine was beginning to putter. I tried to guide her down gently, but the air was thin and she went nose first, plummeting toward the dunes. We managed to secure our parachutes and jumped from the plane and what a sight that was! I tell you, no one has ever truly seen the sunset till he's seen it while hanging from a parachute over the desert. Wasn't that something?

GRANDMA HELMSLEY: Most beautiful, dear.

GRANDPA HELMSLEY: Now where was I? Ah yes, here we are. After landing, we located our plane, salvaged what we could from the wreckage, and set up camp. We weren't sure what we were going to do and we didn't get much sleep, but the desert stars kept us occupied. Nowhere in the world had we seen such beautiful stars. The following morning, I awoke to a tongue licking me across the face.

GRANDMA HELMSLEY: It wasn't me.

GRANDPA HELMSLEY: No! It was a camel—a camel alarm clock. Certainly set the tone for the day. But it truly was most fortunate because that camel belonged to a group of Bedouins who offered to help. We gathered our belongings and—

A PHONE RINGS AND GRANDMA HELMSLEY ANSWERS

GRANDMA HELMSLEY: Hello . . . Yes . . . Oh Richard, that's wonderful news!

GRANDPA HELMSLEY: What's going on?

GRANDMA HELMSLEY: Hold on, let me tell your father. It's a boy. They had a boy—Archer Benjamin.

GRANDPA HELMSLEY: Archer B. Helmsley? Has a nice ring to it.

FOOTSTEPS RUNNING FROM THE ROOM / GRANDMA HELMSLEY STILL ON PHONE

GRANDMA HELMSLEY: We won't stay long. But we do have something we've wanted to ask you.

FOOTSTEPS OF GRANDPA HELMSLEY RETURNING / GRANDMA HELMSLEY HANGS UP

GRANDMA HELMSLEY: We have to go. They're in room thirty-seven E at Rosewood Hospital. What are you—why are you holding that box?

GRANDPA HELMSLEY: They're Richard's old books from school.

GRANDMA HELMSLEY: . . .

GRANDPA HELMSLEY: Thought I'd read to him. He'll get bored staring at the ceiling all day.

GRANDMA HELMSLEY: There won't be time for that, dear; now put those down. How do you turn this thing off? No, it's that one there—the one on the right—no? Try that one then—that's it.

TAPE END

Archer sat quietly, staring at the machine. He heard something familiar in his grandfather's voice. But perhaps that only made sense. He was a Helmsley after all, like Archer's father and Archer himself. And whatever it was about that voice, it sounded wonderful. Both did.

Archer leaned back in the chair.

If they could survive a plane crash in the desert, he thought, *would an iceberg be so bad? Maybe the Eye Patch was right.*

As Archer ejected the tape and stood up to leave, he spotted a wooden box beneath the table. He ran his fingers through the dust and discovered the initials R.B.H. Those were his father's initials. *It can't be the same box.* But sure enough, he lifted the lid and found that it was filled with books. He sat down again, wiped the spines clean, and opened a book titled *The Wind in the Willows*. It was very good. It reminded him of his house.

Archer carried the box upstairs to his room where he moved on to *Gulliver's Travels, Journey to the Center of the Earth, Treasure Island,* and *Alice's Adventures in Wonderland.*

It took Archer only a few days to read all of these books, and his mother left him alone as he did, glad to see he was doing something sensible. Of course, she might have thought otherwise had she bothered looking at the titles.

When he finished *Alice's Adventures in Wonderland,* Archer

set it down and slid off his bed. A door at one end of his room gave way to a balcony and he stepped outside.

• Archer's Decision •

There was a secret world behind the houses on Willow Street. Trees sprouted from the ground, and each house had a walled-in garden and a balcony on the top floor overlooking it. From here, Archer often spied on the neighbors. He leaned against the railing and looked down into the gardens.

A wonderland, he was thinking. *I need to find a rabbit's hole.*

But the only holes in the city were sewer holes, and he couldn't imagine there was much of a wonderland down there.

Still, as he stood there, quietly staring across the gardens, Archer made a decision. He decided he wasn't going to sit around anymore. He was going to figure out a way to escape that tall, skinny house on Willow Street and find an adventure of his own. He had to. After all, Archer was a Helmsley, and being a Helmsley meant something. Archer knew what it meant. It meant he had to do something great—something worthy of the Helmsley Golden Age—something that could even *restore* the Helmsley Golden Age. He knew it wouldn't be easy, but he couldn't let the Helmsleys be reduced to stamp lickers. What would his grandparents say if they knew that? No, he was going to find an adventure that would make them proud. And because his grandparents couldn't help him, he would find someone who could.

Little did he know that the very boy he would ask lived just next door. That boy's name was Oliver J. Glub, and at that very moment, Oliver was sitting on *his* balcony trying to see how many blueberries he could stuff into his mouth. Archer watched closely, guessing Oliver could fit at least twenty, but after number thirteen, he was beginning to have his doubts.

"You're going to explode," called Archer.

Oliver swallowed hard. "That's impossible," he replied.

Despite being neighbors and attending the same school, these were the first words they had ever exchanged.

• Just a Glub •

Archer and Oliver attended the Willow Academy, a school four blocks away, across from Rosewood Park. A long time ago, the Willow Academy had been a Button Factory (and the students still called it that). But after a number of renovations and a fresh coat of paint, it now looked something like a school. Still, great smoke towers loomed high above the roof and Archer sometimes stumbled upon a button, which he added to his collection. It was here, at the Button Factory, that Archer had his second encounter with Oliver.

Oliver was a quiet boy and kept mostly to himself. But if

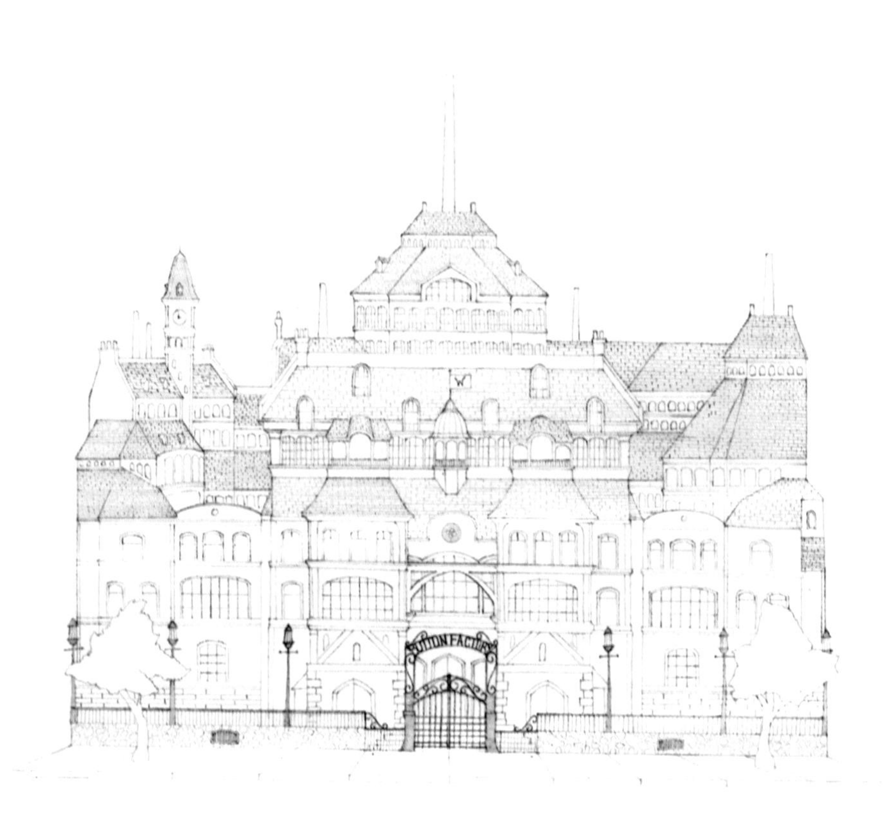

BUTTON FACTORY

51 FOLDINK STREET

you're a quiet boy and keep mostly to yourself, others will often speak for you.

> "He's got a few too many, you know, cracks in his nut," said Charlie H. Brimble.
>
> "He is a nut," said Molly S. Mellings. "And I hope a squirrel takes him away."
>
> "That would never happen," said Alice P. Suggins. "He's one nut no squirrel would want."

It was widely whispered that Oliver was some love child of disaster and tragedy. Perhaps that was true. But Oliver was also unique. And Archer realized this the moment they collided.

"I'm really sorry about that," said Oliver, helping Archer up off the grass. "I didn't see you there."

"I'm not surprised," said Archer. "Do you always run with your eyes closed?"

"Only when I'm late," said Oliver. "When I close my eyes, it feels like I'm running faster."

Archer smiled. He'd never thought about that before.

Although Archer knew very little about Oliver, Oliver knew a great deal about him. Oliver wasn't the only one. Many of the Button Factory students knew a great deal about Archer and his peculiar family.

"They're all crazy," said Alice P. Suggins. "His grandparents are frozen to the side of an iceberg."

"I thought they were eaten by penguins," said Molly S. Mellings. "I know he has penguins inside his house."

"Not just penguins," said Charlie H. Brimble. "There are many strange creatures in Helmsley House—even an Archer."

Archer and Oliver stood in the Button Factory courtyard, next to the crumbling fountain, staring at each other as they had done from their balconies many times. Oliver was a hair taller than Archer (but only because his hair didn't sit flat). He apologized once more and was about to leave, but Archer stuck out his hand.

"My name is Archer Helmsley," he said.

Oliver shook it. "I'm just a Glub," he replied. "My name is Oliver."

"Do you know what a sidekick is?" Archer asked.

Oliver flinched. "Please don't," he said.

After class, Oliver sat on a well-worn couch in the student room listening to Archer recount the story of his grandparents. Oliver pretended this was all news to him, but Oliver knew the story better than most. And while he had no interest in having an adventure or anything of the sort, he was interested in having a friend, so he agreed to help Archer find his adventure if he could.

Besides, he reasoned. *Archer isn't allowed to leave his house. What could possibly happen?*

CHAPTER

THREE

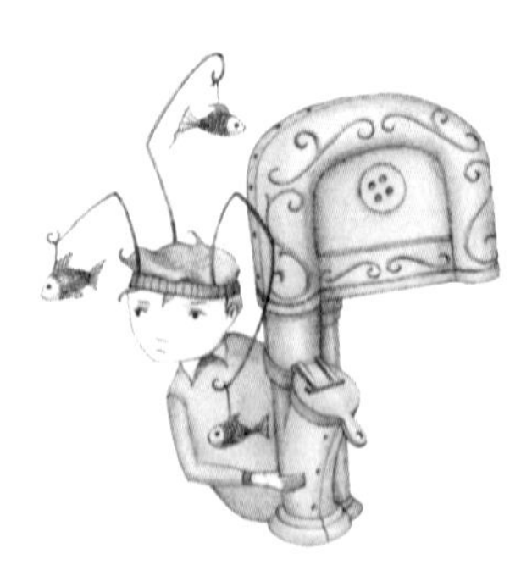

✦ Archer the Submersible ✦

It was the last day of school, but you wouldn't know that from the weather. The rain tapped against the Button Factory windows all afternoon. In a few classrooms, water even dripped from the ceiling and into buckets.

Member of the Rosewood Public Library

Willow Academy Library

• BOOK REQUEST CARD •

Request No. 37953

Miss Whitewood,

Can you please find a few books on the deep sea? I've already read Twenty Thousand Leagues Under the Sea.

Archer Helmsley

When the final bell rang, the students scurried to the exits like mice from a sinking ship. Archer scurried in the opposite direction, up a few flights of stairs, down a number of corridors, in one of which he stopped to pick up a button, and continued to the library.

The Button Factory library was immense. Rows of shelves stretched up to the ceiling with ladders attached so you could reach the top. A separate room was filled with old couches and chairs where students could sit and look out at the inner courtyard. That's where Oliver was waiting, lounging in a big armchair, when Archer stepped inside.

"I've got something good," Archer said.

Oliver looked suspicious and not without reason. According to his math, over the past few weeks Archer had failed to find an adventure more times than he tried. But Oliver wasn't good at math, and it's not possible to fail more times than you try. Still, he was right about one thing. Archer's track record was dismal. Oliver was fine with that.

Archer opened his bag and handed Oliver a mobile made of fish.

"What am I supposed to do with this?" Oliver asked.

"Use the headband," said Archer. "Strap it to your head."

Oliver considered this and then, like any good sidekick, strapped the fish to his head. "Why am I strapping fish to my head?" he asked.

"To set the mood," said Archer.

Miss Whitewood, the school's librarian, rolled by with her pushcart. Of all the teachers at the Button Factory, Archer liked Miss Whitewood the most. She had dark wavy hair and smelled of books.

"Hello, Archer," she said. "I have the books you've requested, but I'm afraid you'll—" She stopped when she saw Oliver.

• Two Weeks Prior •

"Do you have the birdseed?" Archer asked.

Oliver tapped his pockets. Both were filled. "But this is a bad idea. If giant eagles exist, which I'm certain they don't, I'd prefer to stay away from them."

"Trust me," said Archer. "I'll meet you in the library after class and then we'll go to the roof."

Archer sat quietly in the library reading *Twenty Thousand Leagues Under the Sea*. Mrs. Whitewood was atop a ladder shelving books. All at once, the doors flew open and Oliver came barreling down the aisle like a cat on fire.

"Run!" he shouted. "Run!"

Behind him, in hot pursuit, was a flock of chickens, and directly in front of him, Miss Whitewood's ladder. Archer spotted Alice, Charlie, and Molly holding an empty cage and peering proudly through the doorway.

"Open your eyes!" cried Miss Whitewood. "Open your eyes!"

Oliver did, but only in time to see the warning label on the side of the ladder: WARNING: LOCK WHEELS BEFORE MOUNTING, which Miss Whitewood had failed to do.

Oliver smacked the ladder and plopped to the ground. The chickens pounced. Miss Whitewood let out a shriek. The ladder blew clear past the end of the shelf and launched her atop a young girl named Isabella.

One week later, Isabella returned to school. Oliver served his time and repaid his debt to society and Miss Whitewood's limp was now barely noticeable.

✦

"Why does he have fish strapped to his—*no*—never mind. I'm minding my own business." Miss Whitewood turned back to Archer. "As I was saying, I have some books that might help you. But you'll have to leave them here,

I'm afraid. Can't keep books over the summer."

Archer thanked her. Oliver remained silent till Miss Whitewood rolled away.

"Just out of curiosity," he said. "What mood am I setting with these fish strapped to my head?"

Archer was too busy looking through his notebook to hear the question. His fingers were twitching and his eyes were flashing, and though he stood just a few feet from Oliver, Archer was a million miles away.

Oliver waited patiently.

Archer lowered his notebook. "I'm ready," he said.

"Ready for what?"

• World's Greatest Deep-Sea Explorer •

After much deliberation and assessment, Archer had decided he would become the world's greatest deep-sea explorer. He would voyage the vast sweeping seas and penetrate their deepest depths. He would publish journals of his expeditions, cataloging the mutinies and pirate attacks while lost at sea. Man-eating octopi would shudder at the mention of his name—a name that would ring synonymous with the sea. Where Ahab failed, Archer would succeed, capturing as many white whales as historical remembrance required.

Oliver listened closely, and when Archer finished

outlining his next great adventure, he smiled and said, "That sounded really good." And he meant it because it did. "Except for that part where I was swept overboard. I don't see why that was necessary."

Archer reviewed his notes. "I can change that part if you want," he said. "But try not to get caught up in these little details right now."

It was too late for that. Despite his best efforts to indulge Archer's fantasies, Oliver was always caught up in the details. He flipped open a magazine and spoke without looking up.

"What about a ship," he said. "How can you do this without a ship?"

"I'm still working it out," said Archer. But the first step would be to meet in Rosewood Park at midnight and from there, continue on to Rosewood Port. There would probably be a security guard or two at the gate. But if they could slip by unnoticed, the rest would be easy. "We'll just have to pirate a ship and take her to sea."

"Who's going to do that?" Oliver asked, again without looking up.

"We are," said Archer.

"You can operate a boat?"

Archer couldn't operate a boat—an obvious detail he

failed to consider. Then came the submarine. He couldn't operate a submarine, either. In fact, Oliver managed to point out there wasn't a single thing on Archer's list that Archer could do, beginning with step one: *Leave House*.

"Can I take these fish off now?" Oliver asked.

Archer nodded and tore the page from his notebook. He was disappointed, but that was nothing new.

If someone tells you they love turkey smothered with cranberry sauce, that they love it more than anything else in the world, you might spend the day roasting that someone a turkey and smothering it with cranberry sauce. If that same someone then takes one little bite and says, "That'll be all, thank you," you'll likely go red in the face and hurl both these turkeys out the nearest window because clearly, this person never loved turkey smothered with cranberry sauce in the first place.

Little bites are never enough when you love something. When you love something, you want it all. That's how it works. And that's how it was for Archer. Archer didn't want a little taste of adventure with a side of leftover discoveries. Archer wanted the whole turkey and he wanted it stuffed with enough salts and spices to turn his taste buds into sparklers. Needless to say, it was a tall order for a boy who wore a size small blazer.

Archer wrinkled the page into a ball and tossed it into the trash. "Don't worry, I'll figure something out," he said. "I have to."

While Archer was talking, Oliver had come across an ad in the magazine for a shop in Rosewood called Strait of Magellan. The shop sold many things, but the ad was for survival kits. Oliver tore it out and tucked it into his pocket.

"I'm not worried," he said, glancing at the clock. "But we'd better go. You'll be in trouble if you're not home soon."

• All Glubs on Deck •

The sky was still drizzling as they made their way down the sidewalk. The clouds made it feel much later than it was. Archer was watching the streetlamps reflected in puddles. Oliver was staring at the clouds.

"I'd like to be one," he said.

"What's that?" asked Archer.

"A cloud," said Oliver. "I said I'd like to be a cloud."

"Why?"

"Don't you think it'd be nice to be a fluffy white mass looking down on the earth while floating high above it from a safe distance? I think that would be very pleasant."

But these clouds were neither fluffy nor white.

"What about a storm cloud?" asked Archer.

Oliver didn't want to be one of those.

The boys walked up the steps to Oliver's house. Archer wanted his binoculars. Oliver had borrowed them to spy on a new neighbor who'd just moved in across the gardens.

"What's she like?" Archer asked.

"Horrible," said Oliver. "She was shouting at the moon last night, and I think she ate a beetle."

"A *beetle?*"

"Maybe it was just a raisin," Oliver admitted.

They stepped inside the tall green door of house number 377. Oliver dashed up the stairs. Archer sat down on a bench and glanced around the foyer. The Glubs' house always looked as if a giant had picked it up and given it a good shake. And it was styled like a sweater your grandmother knits for you—having too much in the sleeve and too much about the waist but providing more warmth than any other you own. Archer liked it. He didn't have a grandma sweater.

A crash of pots sounded in the kitchen. The door flew open and a mouse scurried across the rug with a look of terror blazing in its beady little eyes. The mouse was followed shortly by Claire, Oliver's younger sister, who chased the creature with a piece of toast hanging from her mouth.

"Afer-noon, Ar-chur!" she cried, and was gone before Archer could reply.

Mrs. Glub poked her frazzled-looking head through the kitchen door. "Get that creature out of the house!" she shouted. "If you don't get that—*oh*, Archer dear—didn't know you were here."

Mrs. Glub took a moment to compose herself, but a composed Mrs. Glub didn't look any different.

"You look wet. Are you hungry? You look hungry. Tea with milk, or toast with jam perhaps?"

"No, thank you," said Archer. "I can't stay."

Mrs. Glub nodded. "Well, you know where to find me if you change your mind," she said. "You mustn't be afraid to speak up."

"Did someone say Archer?" called a voice from upstairs.

It was Mr. Glub.

"*Yes*, someone said *Archer*," Mrs. Glub replied. "But please—the mousetraps!"

Mrs. Glub gave Archer a smile and stepped back into the kitchen. Mr. Glub descended the stairs with the air of a conquering hero. He was a portly fellow who wore weathered suits and had bright blue eyes that were always glad to see Archer.

"Hello, Mr. Glub. How are you?"

Mr. Glub lifted his hands. "You know what they say, Archer. Just bouncing along—bouncing merrily along. Or something along those lines, I suppose."

He popped Archer on the head with a closed fist, a ritual Archer had grown to enjoy.

"You don't look half as excited as Oliver does now that summer's arrived. Two and half months' parole, isn't it?"

For Archer, summer was not two and a half months' parole. It was just the opposite. During school, Archer at least had the Button Factory and the library. During summer, he only had Helmsley House, with very few exceptions.

"You must enjoy being a plump, ripe tomato while you can," Mr. Glub said. "You'll be a sun-dried tomato like me in no time."

This sun-dried tomato was the editor-in-chief of a small newspaper called *The Doldrums Press*. It was not a terribly successful paper by any stretch, but it had a decent, dedicated following. It was *The Doldrums Press*, in fact, that had delivered the iceberg story to Archer's doorstep, and Archer was in the habit of asking Mr. Glub if he'd heard any news about his grandparents.

"Still nothing," Mr. Glub admitted as he pulled on his raincoat and hat. "But there's an expression out there, Archer. Everyone says 'no news is good news.' And while that's bad news for us in the business, in situations like these, it's always for the best, wouldn't you say?"

Archer wasn't sure if no news was for the best in this particular situation, but he nodded all the same.

"I knew them well—your grandparents, I mean," Mr. Glub continued, using Archer's shoulder to balance as he slid into his boots "Ralph once told me we're all explorers, which was a fine observation. The only problem, *I said*, is that a great many of us have embarked on fantastically drab expeditions."

Archer agreed. "My expedition is pretty drab," he said.

Mr. Glub shook his head and opened the front door. "I can't imagine that's true," he replied. "No, I saw that sparkle in your eyes the moment I met you, and I knew it meant something was on the boil. Never told your mother, of course—not sure she goes in for such things. But I was glad to see it. Either way, chin up."

And with that, Mr. Glub shut the door and whistled his way down the rainy sidewalk.

"Found them!" shouted Oliver from atop the stairs. He took the steps three at a time but missed the final few. He valiantly grabbed hold of the railing, spun around, and collapsed in a heap on the floor.

"I hope I didn't break them," he said, handing Archer the binoculars.

"I hope you didn't break yourself," said Archer, helping

him up off the floor. "You have to stop closing your eyes."

"I guess so," Oliver mumbled, dusting his sleeves. "But listen, I was thinking about this whole adventure idea. And before anything else, you should talk to your mother about leaving your house this summer. Otherwise you're not going to get very far. It's been two years. How long are they going to keep you in there?"

Archer hung the binoculars around his neck. "Until I'm too old to walk," he replied.

Oliver grinned. "Well that's only what? Seventy more years at the most."

Archer said good-bye and stepped back into the rain. When he walked up to Helmsley House there was a soggy note on the door.

Archer,

There's been an opossum ravaging the gardens and threatening owners. I'm next door at Mrs. Leperton's. It nearly chewed her ankle off. You're to remain inside the house and out of trouble. I'll be home shortly.

Oliver was right. He had to get permission to leave his house this summer. But it wouldn't be the first time Archer had the discussion with his mother and he knew what she would say: icebergs and *tendencies*. It was hopeless. Still, as he took one last look down Willow Street and shut the door, he was desperate to make it happen.

CHAPTER

FOUR

✦ Doers & Dreamers ✦

Archer was slow getting out of bed. Not for the first time, he'd had a dream that he was the one stuck on the iceberg. He'd wandered the ice in search of the ocean, but frigid peaks shot up all around and no matter how far he traveled, he couldn't find the sea. As always, he awoke before freezing to death and stayed under his covers, waiting till the sunlight made his eyelids glow a brilliant red, then stepped into the bathroom, attached the blindfold to the flamingo, and took a bath.

It was a week into summer, but Archer still had not made the request to leave his house. Today would be the day. Only he wasn't sure how. He and Mrs. Helmsley were very different people.

It's a fact of life that we all dream while we're asleep. Try

as you may, such a thing cannot be avoided. It's when we wake up, however, that we see two types of people emerge. On the one hand are doers, and on the other are dreamers.

When doers wake up, that's it, their dreams are over, and in general, they're content with this. They wash their faces, brush their teeth, and go about their business hoping nothing strange or out of the ordinary will happen along the way. Doers don't do much original thinking and they don't do surprises and they won't ever do anything unexpected or anything someone hasn't already done before. But they are called doers, after all, so they must do *something* and they do. In fact, doers do the same something over and over and over again. This is called routine, and doers are very good at routine.

Dreamers are different.

When dreamers wake up, their dreams have only just begun. They wash their faces and brush their teeth and open the front door hoping everything strange and out of the ordinary is waiting for them. Dreamers like asking questions that have never been asked before and doing things that have never been done before in ways that no one has ever thought of before.

Archer was a dreamer. That was obvious. Even a pigeon somewhere in Rosewood knew that. Mrs. Helmsley was a doer.

✦ Sip of Relief ✦

Archer made his way into the kitchen and ate his breakfast of tea with milk and toast with jam. He listened closely to the advice of his spoon, clanking the side of his cup, as he stirred in the sugar. "Chin up," it said. "You'll be out of here soon." He was plotting just that when his mother entered, her arms filled with groceries. Mr. Helmsley's head was buried in a newspaper.

"I've invited the new neighbors to dinner tonight," Mrs. Helmsley announced. "Murkley—that's their last name. I just met Mrs. Murkley on the sidewalk. She seems a little, well . . . I'm sure both her and her husband are lovely people."

Lovely? thought Archer. After everything Oliver had told him about Mrs. Murkley, *lovely* was not a word he would use.

Mr. Helmsley lowered his newspaper and took a swig of coffee. He didn't look terribly excited, either.

"What time are these *murky* people arriving?" he asked.

Archer smiled. That was the exact word he would use.

Mrs. Helmsley was less amused.

"It's *Murkley*," she said. "They'll be here at seven. And Archer, I expect you to put your best foot forward tonight."

"That would be the left foot," Mr. Helmsley said, raising

his newspaper once more. "Make it eight. I'm in meetings till seven."

Mrs. Helmsley nodded and pointed a bundle of Russian white asparagus at Archer. "First impressions are *most* important," she insisted. "We don't need to review your past performances, do we? She won't admit it, but I'm certain Mrs. Leperton is *still* afraid to come over here."

Archer sighed. While it was true he nearly set Mrs. Leperton on fire during a dinner party a few years back, it was untrue that he did so on purpose. It was simply his first time trying to light candles.

> "But he used the entire matchbook, Helena! And when it ignited, he threw it on my lap!"

No, there was no need for review. Archer was well aware of past dinner parties, which was why he wanted nothing to do with this one. He pressed his tea for advice but the cup was empty, leaving Archer flying solo.

"I'll just stay upstairs," he said, hoping that would put an end to it.

It didn't.

"That would defeat the purpose," his mother replied. "I've invited her to meet you."

"Why?" Archer asked, not sure if he wanted to know the answer.

"She'll be teaching at Willow Academy this fall. She used to teach up at Raven Wood. And I'd like her to meet you. *Oh*, don't make that face. You need good influences!"

"But I'm not feeling well," he lied.

"You're sick?" asked Mr. Helmsley.

"He's not sick."

"I feel sick."

"Then you had better get some rest before they arrive," she said, and that was that. When Mrs. Helmsley put her foot down, she never left an inch of wiggle room.

Archer poked a finger at his toast and thought this over. Perhaps this was an opportunity. Perhaps he could use this to his advantage. It was worth a shot. He turned to his mother and said matter-of-factly, "I'd like to leave the house this summer."

Mrs. Helmsley dropped the asparagus.

"To go to Rosewood Park with Oliver," he quickly added.

"I don't see why not," said Mr. Helmsley from behind the paper. "I see nothing here about iceberg sightings in Rosewood Park."

"It's not a joke," Mrs. Helmsley said.

"I work in law. A sense of humor is required. Just

yesterday a man came in wanting to sue his dog."

"You can't sue a dog," said Archer.

"No," Mr. Helmsley admitted. "But he was fed up with the creature burying the family's fine silver in the backyard."

Mrs. Helmsley stood silently at the sink, rinsing off the asparagus. Archer watched her from the corner of his eye. He was almost certain something was coming—*something good*? He didn't hold his breath.

The interesting thing was that because Archer had spent much of the past few months buried in books, she thought perhaps his *tendencies* were not quite what they once were. Archer didn't know this, but it explained what followed.

"If there are no *episodes*," she said. "If you can give Mrs. Murkley a *good* first impression, *then* we'll discuss what the summer will look like. But I'm not promising anything."

She didn't have to. That was enough. Archer was practically beaming. He was actually going to be free! He quickly retreated from the kitchen before he could ruin this. "Your best foot," she yelled after him, but Archer was already up the stairs.

• Elephant House •

Archer stepped into his closet and scanned the secret boxes. He removed number 17: Elephant House, sat down on the rug near the balcony doors, and pulled the red string.

ARCHER B. HELMSLEY
375 WILLOW STREET

DEAR ARCHER,

I WROTE THIS TO YOU FROM THE BACK OF AN ELEPHANT. WE WERE IN A SMALL COUNTRY WHERE THE INHABITANTS BUILT THEIR HOUSES ON THE BACKS OF THEM. THEY WERE BEAUTIFUL AND HOSPITABLE PEOPLE AND WELCOMED US TO STAY AWHILE. THEY WERE ALSO KIND ENOUGH TO STRAP ME DOWN AT NIGHT. (I HAVE A TENDENCY TO SLEEPWALK.)

A MAN NAMED AYYAPPIN SCULPTED THIS ELEPHANT HOUSE AS A GIFT. THE STONE IS JADE. BEAUTIFUL, ISN'T IT? WE THOUGHT YOU MIGHT LIKE IT.

YOURS TRULY,
Ralph Helmsley

Archer wished Helmsley House had been built on the back of an elephant. Each night he would fall asleep as the elephant wandered, and in the morning he would wake up some place entirely new. But house number 375 was planted firmly on the ground, and the view from his balcony remained completely unchanged.

Archer went to his dresser, clicked on the radio, found his notebook in a drawer, and was thinking about Rosewood

Park as he returned to the rug. He had no intention of staying inside the park. The question was where could he go from there? And he sat quietly, considering just that as the sunlight slanted in through the balcony door. His thoughts were shortly interrupted when a shrill cry shot up from the gardens.

"HENRY!" the voice shouted.

Archer tilted his head.

"HENRY!" the voice shouted again.

Archer grabbed his binoculars and hurried to the balcony.

• Non-Nocturnal Opossum •

Oliver had also dashed to his balcony. Archer motioned to him. Oliver climbed a ladder to the roof, hopped over the small gap between the houses, and slid down the ladder to Archer's balcony.

"What's going on?" he asked.

Archer wasn't sure. He directed his binoculars down into the gardens. The voice that had cried "Henry!" belonged to Mrs. Murkley, a rather bulbous woman with little neck to spare, who at present was cornered by an opossum in her garden.

"HENRY!" she shouted. "HENRY!"

The Murkleys' garden door swung open and a man who

looked in need of a decent meal sauntered valiantly through.

"Yes, my dear?" he said. "What seems to be the—*ah*! What *is* that?"

"It's what you're about to kill!" shouted Mrs. Murkley. "So don't just stand there. Get a shovel and smash it to pieces!"

There are many tunes in this world that can soothe the savage beast. That wasn't one of them. The opossum hunched its back and let out a terrible hiss.

"Don't show it fear," Henry said. "I think they attack when they sense fear."

The opossum turned to Henry and gave him the once-over. Henry backed into the opposite corner of the garden.

"On second thought," he said. "Show it a little fear, darling."

Oliver placed his hand on Archer's shoulder, trying his best not to look afraid. "Opossums don't really attack when they sense fear, do they?" he asked.

"Normal opossums don't," said Archer. "They just play dead." But this opossum was out in the daylight, and Archer thought it might be a non-nocturnal opossum. "I've never seen one out in the day before."

Oliver hadn't, either. "But it looks too soft and fluffy to be violent," he said. "Mrs. Murkley, on the other hand . . ."

With all of her shouting, Mrs. Murkley had gone quite pink in the face and looked something like an overzealous mosquito. The non-nocturnal (and probably nonviolent) opossum eyed both Murkleys. It seemed to realize it was outnumbered and sounded the retreat, scurrying backward up the garden wall and scampering away. As it did, the opossum paused to look up at Archer and Oliver.

"I think that thing just winked at me," said Oliver. "I knew it wasn't violent. Isn't *she* horrible, though?"

Archer pointed his binoculars back toward the Murkley house. The garden was empty.

"She's coming to dinner tonight," he said.

Oliver paled. "That's terrible! Why would your mother invite that?"

"She'll be teaching at the Button Factory this fall."

Oliver needed to sit down for a moment. It was a lot to take in. As he did, Archer explained what else his mother had said and that come tomorrow, they would be on their way to Rosewood Park.

"That place creeps me out," said Oliver. "It's like the city grew around it and no one knew what to do so they left it there."

"We're not going to stay *inside* the park," said Archer. "It's about getting out of *here*. And from Rosewood Park, we can go—anywhere."

"Where's anywhere?" Oliver asked.

Archer wasn't sure. He ducked back inside his room and returned with one of his grandfather's journals. Those were filled with brilliant ideas.

"While you're figuring that out," said Oliver. "You should come to my house."

Delicious smells were wafting from the Glubs' kitchen. Mrs. Glub always made wonderful food. Archer knew this because ever since he'd become friends with Oliver, he'd been sneaking into Oliver's house. His mother had no idea how easy it was, and she was completely unaware how frequently he did it. She wouldn't like it. And with his chance for real freedom so close, perhaps he shouldn't risk it today. But Archer knew a dinner party at night meant a day of busied preparations for his mother. He just had to be careful. So he followed Oliver up the ladder, over the crack between the houses, and down the stairs to the Glubs' kitchen.

• Wonders of Weeding •

Mrs. Glub nearly hit the ceiling when Archer and Oliver stumbled in through the back door to the kitchen.

"Did you take the roof again?" she asked, staring at the both of them.

DOLDRUMS PRESS

Archer and Oliver exchanged glances.

"It's not safe jumping over that gap! One of these days you're going to fall into it and Mr. Glub will have to fish you out!"

"But the roof is quicker," said Oliver, following the delicious smells seeping from the oven.

"Quicker is rarely safer," Mrs. Glub said. "But I'm glad you're here, Archer, and you're just in time. Have a seat."

Mrs. Glub pulled a steaming hot tray of apple cider turnovers from the oven. They were crusted in caramel and nuts and smelled heavenly.

"I'm taking your sister to get a new dress," she said to Oliver. "I need you to weed the garden while we're out. That flower festival, or whatever it's called, is just around the corner." Mrs. Glub frowned. "I'm sure the neighbors are whispering again."

Oliver said he would get to it after eating, and when Mrs. Glub left the house, they began popping apple cider turnovers into their mouths as quickly as they could, careful not to burn their tongues. Archer ate with his head buried inside his grandfather's journal. What *was* he going to do when he left the house?

"They finally opened the new upstairs area at DuttonLick's sweetshop," said Oliver. "Everyone from the Button Factory was going there yesterday. We could go if you can actually leave your house. I think you'd really like the—"

"We should do this," interrupted Archer, not hearing a word Oliver had just said.

. . . the jungle dripped with uncertainty. Everywhere were insects, flying, jumping, and crawling up trees. One bit my arm. A bump swelled, festered, and popped. It flowed yellow. I became delirious. Rachel nursed out the poison and we dug in for the night. The air was thick and the wood, too wet to burn. We floated in a sea of leaves and moss. Large creatures lurked in the moonlight. We couldn't see them, but knew they were near. . . .

Oliver lowered his pastry. His appetite was gone. "I don't understand you sometimes—*a lot* of times. What about that sounds enjoyable?"

"'*Floating in a sea of leaves and moss,*'" said Archer. "Deep in a jungle beneath the moonlight. That's what we should do. That would be wonderful."

Oliver shook his head and the crumbs from his fingers. "Wonderful," he mumbled, jumping down from the counter and leaving the kitchen. Archer followed with a pastry in one hand and the journal still opened in the other.

. . . it was a strange plant. I shouldn't have eaten it. Rachel was right about that. Looked like it might taste good. I was wrong about that. . . .

Oliver and Archer stepped into the garden.

"Well," said Oliver. "There's your sea of leaves and moss."

Archer lowered the journal.

The Glubs' garden was something of a neighborhood scandal. The stone walkway was a slimy green and the walls were caked with ivy. An apple tree that bore no apples was in desperate need of trimming and the grass, if you could call it grass, was at least knee high. The difficult part in weeding such a garden was trying to decide what was a weed and what wasn't because it all looked the same.

"I usually just fill one bag and call it a day," Oliver said.

Archer spotted the ceramic top of something pink only just visible through the grass.

"Is that a flamingo?" he asked.

Oliver nodded. "Dad won it. Mom hates it."

Archer turned to look at the back of Helmsley House. The windows were open, but there was no sign of his mother. *She'll still be in the kitchen*, he thought. He put down the journal on the window ledge and rolled up his sleeves.

"You're helping?" Oliver asked.

"It'll give me time to think," he replied.

Oliver grabbed a garbage bag and they set to work. In no time at all, weeds were flying this way and that. It was a terrific mess and they were covered in dirt. Archer continually looked up at his house until deciding it was safer, not to mention easier, to stay out of sight next to the garden wall. Oliver was struggling against a stubborn weed when he noticed the tip of the flamingo had vanished.

"What happened to the flamingo?" he asked. "You didn't weed the flamingo by mistake, did you?"

Archer didn't and nearly tripped over a rock while saying so. He pushed aside the grass with his shoe and discovered a moss-covered stone with the name "Théo" etched into it.

"Who's Théo?" he asked.

Oliver released the stubborn weed and fell backward onto some slimy stones.

"I'd rather not talk about it," he said, picking himself up. "You wouldn't believe me anyway."

When they'd finished, Archer couldn't tell if the garden looked better or worse. Oliver shrugged. It always looked the same to him. As they piled weeds into the garbage bag, two voices floated over the garden wall. It wasn't the Murkleys. Archer pointed at the apple-less apple tree. They climbed the trunk and peered diagonally into the garden just opposite Archer's where a short woman in a flowered dress, carrying a clipboard and a cup of coffee, ushered a tall, well-groomed man out through the garden doors. Archer was surprised to see anyone there. No one lived in that house.

• A Tall, Well-Groomed Man •

The flowery woman finished the last of her coffee and handed the cup, without looking, to the tall, well-groomed man.

"And this is the garden," she said, peeling her eyes from the clipboard. "Oh! Isn't it lovely—just so lovely, isn't it? Always wished I had a garden so lovely. Never, though—never in my life have I had a garden so lovely. The lovely flowers and the lovely trees, and look! There are two lovely boys in that one. A boy tree? I've never seen such a lovely boy tree!"

Archer and Oliver quickly hid themselves behind more branches.

"Her eyes look strange," Oliver whispered.

Archer agreed.

The flowery woman's eyes were white all around with beady black dots at the centers, which made them think she'd spent the afternoon staring at the sun.

"Or was struck by lightning," whispered Archer.

The tall, well-groomed man was staring up at the back of the house and spoke with a funny accent.

"It's as lovely as you promised," he said. "But it will require a few *minor alterations* before we move across the sea. I want my daughter to feel at home here."

"Across the sea?" whispered Archer.

"Daughter?" whispered Oliver.

The flowery woman rapidly bobbed her head. "Oh, yes—yes of course. Anything you need—anything at all. I'll put you in touch with a man—two lovely men! They can do anything you need. Anything you want, they'll do. Yes, wonderful, very good indeed. We've found you a new house—a lovely, lovely house!"

The man grinned. "Another espresso?" he asked. "Or a double perhaps?"

The woman's eyes grew even beadier. "You can make a *double*?" she replied.

They disappeared back inside the lovely, lovely house.

"We're getting another new neighbor?" said Oliver.

Archer was about to respond, but his train of thought was interrupted when he caught sight of Mrs. Murkley over the other wall. She was barreling out through her garden door with a shovel raised high above her head.

"IT'S BACK, HENRY!" she shouted. "THAT CREATURE IS IN THAT TREE!"

Archer reeled backward and fell to the ground. Oliver froze. Mrs. Murkley brought the shovel down with terrific force. It crunched through the branches and sliced one in half just next to Oliver's head. He lost his balance. The ceramic flamingo broke his fall and shattered to pieces. Mrs. Murkley cheered from the other side.

"I GOT IT!" she cried. "I KILLED THAT HORRIBLE CREATURE!"

The gardens fell silent once more as two lumps of boy struggled for air beneath the tree. Archer had rolled against the garden wall, fearing his mother had overheard the commotion. Oliver stared at him in disbelief.

"She nearly chopped my head off!" said Oliver, sitting up and pulling a piece of flamingo from his hair. "She's not really going to dinner at your house, is she?"

Archer nodded. In a few short hours, he would be breaking bread with that woman. Oliver stumbled to his feet and offered him a hand.

"I should go," Archer said.

"You better hope she leaves the shovel at home," said Oliver.

"I'll worry about that," he replied. "You just make sure you're ready for tomorrow."

But when Archer returned to his room, the excitement of what tomorrow might bring was squeezed out by concerns about that night's festivities. "*My best foot,*" he repeated over and over as he put on a new green velvet suit and secured a red bow tie to his collar.

CHAPTER

FIVE

✦ A Stole in Summer ✦

That evening, fifteen minutes prematurely, the doorbell rang. Mr. Helmsley was upstairs, trying to remove cologne he'd been heavy-handed in applying, and Archer was sitting at the table, half-watching as Mrs. Helmsley moved frantically about the kitchen. He had offered to help but his mother wanted everything perfect, so Archer sat quietly in his bow tie, keeping himself busy with his grandfather's journal, which he held just out of sight.

. . . the train was green—a brilliant green. There were no seats inside. We climbed and sat atop the roof. A fine choice that was. The twisting mountains were incredible. . . .

When the doorbell rang, Mrs. Helmsley was in the middle of slicing a roasted lamb and sent Archer to welcome the Murkleys.

"And remember what I told you," she said (the knife in her hand made her look very serious). "Be sure to say 'thank you' and 'yes, ma'am' and 'no, ma'am.' And don't forget to introduce yourself: 'My name is Archer.'"

Archer inched his way down the hall. The sitting room canary grew silent. He reached for the knob but before he could even touch it, the door flew open and in tramped Mrs. Murkley followed shortly by Henry. Archer was speechless and, if only for a brief second, thoughtless. He stared at Mrs. Murkley. Mrs. Murkley stared back at him.

Seeing Mrs. Murkley from a balcony or a tree was one thing. From this angle, her figure bore a striking resemblance to a hot air balloon. He made an educated guess, however, that this lady would never float so gracefully off the ground.

Finally, Mrs. Murkley broke the silence.

"Young man," she snorted. "My coat—you should offer to take my coat!"

Archer tried to say something, but he was rattled and nothing came out. Any word would have been better than nothing, but nothing was all he had. Then, his mother's instructions flashed through his head.

"Thank you," he said.

"Why are you thanking me?" she snipped.

"Yes, ma'am," he replied.

"Yes what?"

"No, ma'am."

"What's wrong with you?"

"My name is Archer," said Archer.

It was a terrible thing to see Archer go to pieces like this, but there was something in Mrs. Murkley's gaze that simply undid him. Mrs. Murkley turned that gaze to Henry.

"I'm going to drop my coat on it," she whispered. "Keep your distance—don't let it touch you."

Archer stuck out his arms. Mrs. Murkley dropped her coat and proceeded to the dining room. Henry followed close behind. Mr. Helmsley hurried down the stairs while tucking in his shirt and nodded at Archer.

"A *fur* coat?" he whispered as he passed by. "What kind of person wears fur in the summer?"

Archer had a few guesses, but his knees were about to give out. He quickly reached for one of the two caribous that the Helmsleys used as coatracks.

"Not mine!" cried the first. "Use his. My antlers can't support that kind of weight."

Archer turned to the second caribou.

"That's absolute rubbish!" it replied. "His antlers are much stronger than mine!"

"I'm sorry, but I have to," Archer said, hooking the coat on the first.

No sooner did he let go than the antler point snapped, dropping the coat in a heap on the floor.

"Look what you've done!" the caribou cried.

Archer picked up the antler point and tucked it into his pocket, promising to fix it after dinner. He left the coat where it was and quickly made for the dining room.

• A Difficult Pea to Swallow •

Of all the rooms in Helmsley House, the dining room was truly something special. Circling the table were animals from all four corners of the world. A zebra, peacock, and antelope stood among many others. Archer took his usual spot in front of the antelope. Mrs. Murkley was directed to the seat next to him. *Lovely*.

During dinner, Archer paid little attention to the conversation. Even if he had been interested, he knew his opinion wouldn't matter. All that concerned him was keeping his mouth shut and his best foot forward. He chased a pea around the plate with his fork.

Mrs. Murkley's eyes took a turn about the room as she hacked away at her lamb. "What did you say you do for a living?" she asked Mr. Helmsley. "Perfume sales, was it?"

"I'm a lawyer," Mr. Helmsley replied. "But if you're wondering about the house, it's my parents' doing. Ralph and Rachel Helmsley. They were explorers. Perhaps you've heard of them?"

Mrs. Murkley had never heard of them and she was glad because she had no interest in people who gallivant the world aimlessly. After saying this, she continued staring at the animals.

"They certainly are a little, you know, *out there*," she said. "I could never share a house with such people."

"They don't live here anymore," said Mrs. Helmsley.

"There was an iceberg incident," said Mr. Helmsley.

Mrs. Murkley nodded. "That's pretty far out there," she said. "But what can one expect from people who make such bizarre career choices?"

Archer pressed his pea-chasing fork hard against his plate. It made a terribly unpleasant screech. Mrs. Murkley glared at him.

"Are you having utensil troubles, Alfred?" she asked.

"My name is Archer," said Archer, and he wasn't having utensil problems. He was having a brash-behemoth-insulting-his-grandparents problem.

"Are you sure?" Mrs. Murkley insisted. "Because you've been trying to secure that pea for quite some time now. Or perhaps it's distaste for the vegetable that drives your fork to wander. Either way, end this wild goose chase and eat that pea."

Archer didn't mind eating peas, but doing something because you wish to is different from doing something because you're told to. Still, he could feel his mother eyeing him from across the table and he knew what he had to do. Archer begrudgingly swallowed the pea. Mrs. Murkley turned back to the adults and smiled.

"It's a gift," she chirped. "One that I discovered when I was still quite little. When I instruct, people listen. I see what's wrong and I fix it. Take this room for example," she said, using her fork as a pointer. "I know someone who can fix this terrible mess that Ralph and Rachel have left you with."

She's the one who needs fixing, thought Archer.

Mr. Helmsley smiled. "There does seem to be something off about it," he said. "I just haven't been able to put my finger on it."

Mrs. Helmsley nudged him.

"That's just it!" Mrs. Murkley squealed. "And this is *precisely* why I teach children. Now you mustn't take this personally, Richard, but old minds are far too rusty and corroded to change their ways. Young minds, on the other hand, are *ripe* for adjustment. The modus operandi is really not so different from that of a mechanic. One simply sticks a wrench into their little ear and twists the bolts till you have them running smoothly—metaphorically speaking, of course," she quickly added.

She's not sticking that wrench in my ear, thought Archer.

"I don't think it's too much to assume," Mrs. Murkley continued, "that things could have been much different for Ralph and Rachel had they known someone like me when they were little. Yes, I could have set them straight just like young Alfred here."

"That certainly would have been interesting," Mr. Helmsley replied.

Archer didn't find this interesting in the least. Who did this balloon think she was to come into Helmsley House and insult the very people who created it? No, she couldn't have changed his grandparents and she wouldn't control him. As the adults continued the conversation, Archer put his best foot under the chair and began slipping his peas, one by one, into his hand.

"And what made you decide to leave Raven Wood?" Mr. Helmsley asked.

Mrs. Murkley took a gulp of wine. "You know how it is with these schools," she said. "Always changing personnel.

Sometimes I feel like a missionary of old, going from one jungle to the next."

When Archer had gathered a generous amount of peas, he discreetly reached back to discard them into the antelope's mouth.

"I don't want those, either," said the antelope.

"But you're a herbivore," whispered Archer.

"Even we herbivores have our limits."

Despite its protest, the antelope soon found Archer's hand inserted into its mouth. But just as Archer was about to make the deposit, a shadow from the east fell upon him.

"And what's this!" demanded Mrs. Murkley.

A pea shot from her mouth and landed safely in Henry's eye.

Archer froze.

"Remove that hand!" she persisted, but Archer kept it where it was.

The air congealed. Henry retrieved the pea so he could see what was happening.

"Archer Helmsley, remove that hand *at once*!" Mrs. Helmsley demanded.

Archer instantly regretted putting himself in this position. Everyone was staring at him, but he mostly looked at his mother. She wasn't going to like this. Not one bit. He slowly removed his hand. The antelope gave a sigh of relief. Mrs. Murkley grabbed his wrist. Peas bounced in all directions. Henry's eye caught a second one.

"Just as I thought," Mrs. Murkley announced. "It would appear, Helena, that your son has been using this late gazelle's mouth as a hiding spot for his unwanted vegetables."

"It's not a gazelle," said Archer, pulling his wrist free. "It's an antelope."

"Yes," agreed Henry. "If you'll note how the antlers—"

"I don't care what kind of animal it is," Mrs. Murkley bellowed. "I *do* know it's not a trash can."

Archer cringed as his mother tried her best to retrieve the wayward peas. This was going to ruin everything if he didn't find a way to quickly make up for it.

"I apologize to you both," Mrs. Helmsley said. "This is *not* the sort of behavior we expect from him."

"I should hope not," said Mrs. Murkley, plopping a potato into her mouth. "I will not tolerate such behavior from my students at the academy and I warn you both right now, should Alfred keep this up, I wouldn't be surprised if he ends up in prison."

"Prison?" said Henry.

"Prison?" Mr. Helmsley smiled.

"Yes, *prison*," said Mrs. Murkley.

I'm already in prison, thought Archer.

"I'll bet if you asked around," said Mrs. Murkley, "you would find that many criminals began their slippery slope into a life of crime by stuffing their unwanted vegetables into the mouths of animals."

"Into her mouth, more like it," whispered the antelope.

Archer smiled, but that was another mistake. Mrs. Murkley caught sight of this and thought he was smiling at her. Mrs. Murkley was not the sort of woman you smile at. A tiny vein on her temple doubled in size, and her face turned as red as the wine in her glass.

"Go right ahead and laugh, young man!" she snapped, throwing her napkin on the table. "By all means, everyone laugh! Just don't expect an ounce of sympathy from me when the police pound at your door and sentence him to the electric chair as punishment for his life of crime!"

Archer looked at his father.

"Why don't you go on upstairs," Mr. Helmsley said. "We'll discuss this later."

"We certainly will," said Mrs. Helmsley, who in that moment looked more frightening than Mrs. Murkley.

Without protest, Archer stood up and did as he was told, avoiding eye contact with his mother as he made for the door. Just before leaving, he turned back to Mrs. Murkley, planning to apologize, but Mrs. Murkley cut him off.

"You watch it, young man," she said. "Or you just might find yourself atop an iceberg someday."

• Heat Rises •

It's often said that heat rises, and it must be true because Archer was feeling hot under the collar when he reached the top of the stairs. It's not difficult to see why. If some brash behemoth marched into your house and told your parents that one day you'd be sitting cozy in an electric chair, you might be tempted to lower an eyebrow or two. But that wasn't it. It was the comments about his grandparents being crazy that set Archer boiling.

Did Ralph and Rachel march to the beat of a different drum? Perhaps. You could even say they ditched the marching and the drums and danced a jig to a xylophone instead. But crazy? Certainly not. Ralph and Rachel never wore fur in the summer.

Archer ripped off his bow tie and tossed it to the floor. He trudged down the hallway to his bedroom knowing tomorrow would not bring something new. Tomorrow would bring something worse. And he now wanted nothing more than to drive that beastly woman out of Helmsley House.

"Be on the lookout," he said to the polar bear in the alcove. "If what they say about heat rising is true, there's a hot air balloon that's sure to come this way. And she'll look at you as if *you're* the bizarre museum creature."

"But I am the bizarre museum creature," the polar bear replied.

"You're more real than she is!"

No sooner did Archer say these words than he was struck with a brilliant idea. A smile stretched across his face and he turned back to the polar bear.

"You're much bigger than a non-nocturnal opossum," he said.

"Please don't drag me into this," the bear replied.

But that's precisely what Archer did. With all his might, he dragged the bear down the hallway and into his bedroom. Archer would have his revenge.

✦ No More Than an Hour Later ✦

Archer was no stranger to Helmsley House dinner parties. And he knew that almost anyone who ever attended one would request a tour of the house. These tours always concluded near his bedroom on the top floor. That's what he was hoping for and, sure enough, no more than an hour later, voices were heard ascending the stairs.

"And this, Henry, is our—" Mr. Helmsley stopped. "Where's the polar bear?"

Mrs. Helmsley shook her head. "What polar bear?" she asked.

"There was a polar bear here."

"I never noticed a polar bear."

Henry nodded. "Polar bears are like that sometimes."

"Enough with the polar bears!" Mrs. Murkley demanded. "If it found these living arrangements *half* as disturbing as I do, it's likely that creature took the first bus out of here. Now please, I've seen far more than I care to see and it's time we returned home."

Mrs. Murkley marched back to the stairs, but Mrs. Helmsley stopped her retreat. She had only dragged Mrs. Murkley along because she wanted Archer to apologize for his behavior in the dining room and for leaving her coat in a heap on the floor. Mrs. Murkley sighed and made the universal gesture for *let's get on with it then*. She pushed her way to the front of the group and pointed to a door. Mrs. Helmsley nodded.

"Right," huffed Mrs. Murkley, and she threw it open.

Revenge is a dish best served cold, but you mustn't go too cold. Archer went too cold. After waiting an hour, Archer had fallen asleep. What's worse, he had fallen asleep in the very trap he'd set for Mrs. Murkley. That is to say, he fell asleep with his head inside the gaping jaws of the retired polar bear. His body drooped on a chair.

When Mrs. Murkley threw open the door, it collided with the wall, jolting Archer from his dream and into a situation he didn't remember. He saw teeth. He felt fur. He panicked.

Archer shouted. The glass eye fell from the bear's mouth and rolled across the floor. It bounced off Mrs. Murkley's shoe and looked up at her. Mrs. Murkley's shriek was of such a pitch and volume that it would have buried them all beneath an avalanche had they been living in the Himalayas. Henry fell backward down the stairs. Mr. Helmsley failed to grab him. Mrs. Helmsley was a blank slate (likely saving her expressions for later). Archer braced, thinking the walls were about to implode. Fortunately, Mrs. Murkley imploded first.

• One Part Hand & Two Parts Butter •

Archer stood on the front steps, watching as the paramedics carried Mrs. Murkley out of the house on a stretcher. He was still foggy as to what had just happened.

"A criminal," she mumbled as she passed. "That's what you are! That's what you've raised!"

"I can't apologize to you enough for this dinner," his mother said.

"No need for that," said Henry, hoisting himself into

the back of the ambulance. He tapped at his chest where presumably a heart was located. "Bad ticker," he said. "She's had a bad one ever since she was little. Nothing to worry about." He lowered his voice to a whisper. "She's a little dramatic about it."

"Stand clear," said a paramedic as he slammed the doors. "Stand clear."

With sirens blaring, the ambulance sped off down Willow Street bound for Rosewood Hospital. Whatever remaining hope Archer had of seeing anything but the inside of Helmsley House that summer was also rushed off to the hospital. Unlike Mrs. Murkley, such hope would not survive the night.

Archer stuck his hands in his blazer pockets.

"I'm sorry," he said. "I fell asleep."

"And it's time you wake up!" Mrs. Helmsley demanded. "You're buttering your grip on reality!"

"I guess the best foot was the right foot," Mr. Helmsley mumbled. "Well, nowhere to go except up. I suppose there's always sideways, but I think up would be preferable. Regardless, I think we'll agree that she was a little, you know, *out there*."

"That's no excuse!"

Archer could feel the heat pouring off his mother. He'd

seen her angry before, but not like this. You could probably fry an egg on her head, but now wasn't a good time to attempt such a thing. Archer had wanted to drive Mrs. Murkley out of Helmsley House. He didn't intend to do so with an ambulance. But that's what had happened. And after he followed his parents back inside, the swift arm of justice fell and it fell *hard*.

CHAPTER SIX

• A Change of Scenery •

Helmsley House was never a loud place, but it was especially quiet in the weeks that followed the polar bear incident. There are always exceptions, but in general, sending someone to the hospital is frowned upon in a civil society.

During those weeks, the door to Archer's room was locked except when a tray of food was brought in. For a while, that tray contained leftovers from the Murkley dinner party, forcing Archer to relive that night over and over again. Why had he been so foolish? Archer stretched out across his bed and tried reading his grandfather's journals, but he kept putting them down. Oliver stopped by one morning and convinced Archer to sneak over to his house. Archer was glad he did.

"He's innocent!" cried Claire.

"Of course he is," said Mr. Glub, placing his hands on

Archer's shoulders. "Perhaps not in the classical sense, but she had no right to come into your house and insult your grandparents as she did. I've never met anyone who had something bad to say about Ralph and Rachel."

"I think she likes to argue," said Oliver.

Mrs. Glub agreed and slid an apple cider turnover in front of Archer. "You'll always find trouble if you go looking for it."

Archer was glad to have the Glubs' support, but he wished his parents would take a similar stance. They didn't.

One evening, when the door to his room was finally unlocked, Archer joined his parents for dinner, but there was little chewing of the fat. Everyone was chewing on something else. Mrs. Helmsley looked at him with an expression similar to the one she made while smelling the milk to see if it was still safe to drink.

"You'll be putting all of this nonsense behind you," she said. "One more incident like that—I do mean *one more*—and I'll be contacting Raven Wood. These outbursts—these *tendencies*—they're dangerous! And they end *now*!"

Even Mr. Helmsley didn't argue.

Archer didn't know much about Raven Wood except that it was a boarding school three hours north of Rosewood by train. To one side, the school was shrouded in thick pines and to the other was a rocky beach and the same sea that bordered Rosewood. Archer told Oliver Raven Wood was the school Mrs. Murkley had left. And though she never said why, both agreed it didn't say much about the institution.

"I'll bet all the teachers there are like her," said Oliver.

Archer tried his best to be extra careful around his mother. It's a curious thing, however, that when you're trying to be extra careful, you always end up doing something careless. Archer was no exception. And one day, Archer did something careless. He left his secret bookshelf uncovered when his mother came in with freshly ironed shirts and socks.

"What are all of these boxes?" she asked.

Archer jumped to his feet with such haste that his heart ended up somewhere around his left ankle.

"Nothing!" he said, trying to usher her out. "They're nothing!"

Mrs. Helmsley wouldn't budge. She bent down and removed a box.

"Are these from . . . ? But how did *you* . . . ? How did *they* . . . ?"

Archer paled. "Those aren't mine," he said, not sure what else to say.

His mother eyed him. "They have *your* name on them."

Archer slumped down on the edge of his bed. Mrs. Helmsley began grabbing packages left and right and didn't stop till her arms were full and the shelves were empty. She took the journals, too. Only the glass eye dared an escape. When she reached the door, it fell from the stack and rolled over to Archer's foot. He kicked it under the bed.

"We'll talk about this later," she said. But days went by and it was never mentioned again.

There was only one time Archer could remember feeling more miserable and that was the morning he discovered the iceberg headline. But there was a small reprieve in the midst of all this. Construction began on the house just opposite him. And it began very early one morning.

• Minor Alterations •

Archer leaned against his balcony railing in his pajamas and stared across the way. For the first time, he didn't recognize his view. The house across the gardens (the house where he'd seen the flowery woman and the tall, well-groomed man) was now covered in scaffolding. Workers climbed up and down ladders at a frantic pace shouting:

> "Be careful." "Lift with your back." "That's it."
> "That can't be right." "Is it supposed to look like that?"

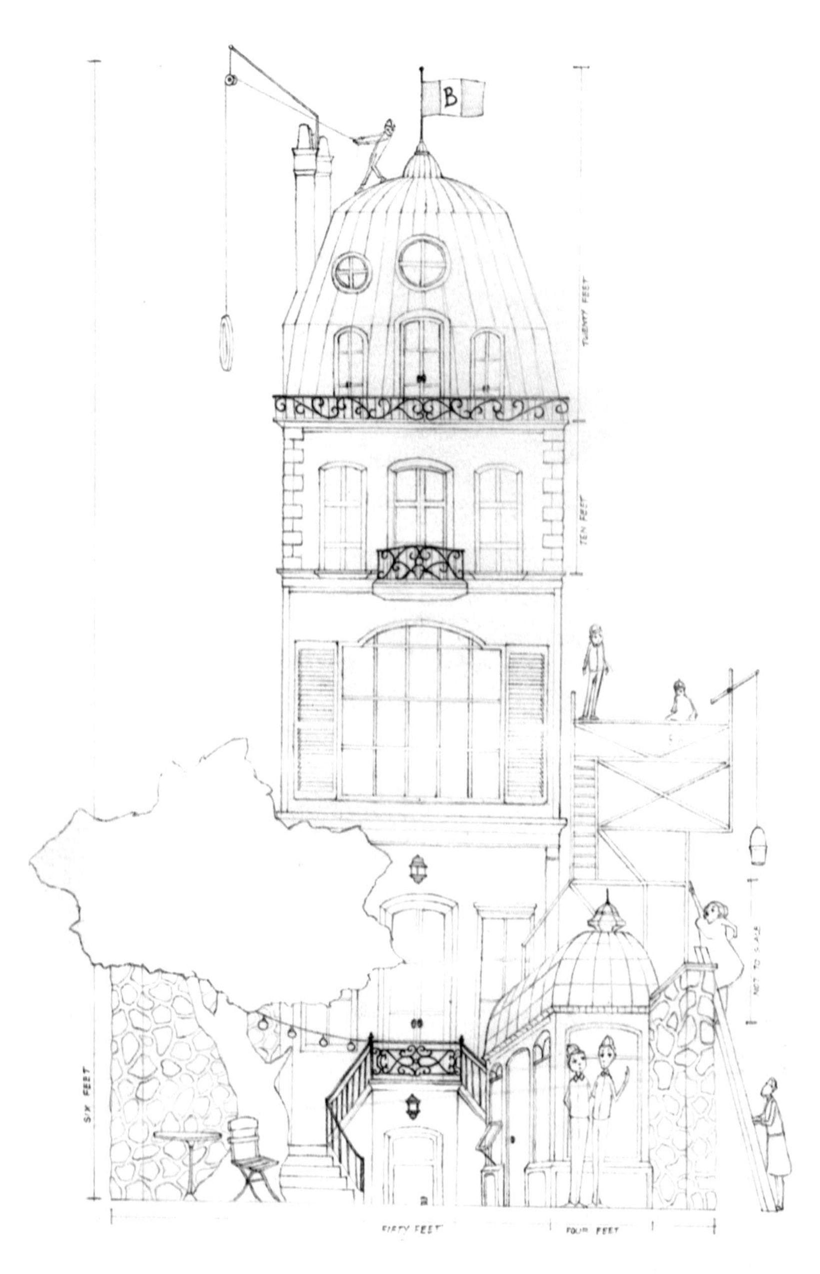

PARISIAN BROWNSTONE

376 NORTH WILLOW STREET

Oliver jumped out on his own balcony and yelled, "What's going on!"

Archer couldn't hear him over the noise. He motioned and Oliver climbed the ladder to join him.

"Good morning," Archer mumbled.

"This is not a good morning," said Oliver, who just moments before had leaped from his bed thinking the world was coming to an end.

Down below, Mrs. Murkley stormed out through the garden door followed by Henry, who was carrying a ladder. It was clear she'd made a full recovery from the polar bear incident and was back to her cheery self. Archer boiled just looking at her. She snatched the ladder from her husband, propped it up against the wall, and when she reached the top, began barking at the workers. Henry, who was still in his bathrobe and slippers, disappeared back inside.

"What's the meaning of all this!" Mrs. Murkley growled.

The construction stopped. A man approached the wall and handed her what looked like a business card.

"Good morning," he said cheerfully. "My name is Pierre."

A second man approached and handed her a second business card.

"My name is also Pierre," he said.

After that, they spoke in unison.

"We're the brothers Pierre, home remodelers at your service."

Mrs. Murkley studied one Pierre and then the other. "You're a circus act is what you are," she said, and threw the cards over their heads. "Have you any idea what time it is?"

One Pierre looked up at the sun. The other Pierre looked down at his watch. They reached the same conclusion.

"Seven in the morning," both said.

"But the sooner we're here," said Pierre number one.

"The sooner we can leave," said Pierre number two.

"This is weird," said Oliver.

Archer agreed.

Mrs. Murkley pointed at the scaffolding. "If even so much as one little piece of *anything* falls into my garden . . . I'll make sure the police are ready for you! Henry, get the phone! Henry?" She turned but Henry was gone. "Useless man!" The workers laughed. "Keep laughing, you fools! You'll see what happens!"

The construction lasted a number of weeks and while the noise was constant, Archer didn't mind because it muffled his sorrows. He stood near the balcony door with his binoculars raised, watching as Mrs. Murkley checked for garden debris. She was rather like a mole popping its head from its subterranean lair to gander at the happenings of the aboveground dwellers. There was no debris. But there was a great deal of dust. And that dust ruined the summer flower festival. Mrs. Helmsley was furious when her flowers bloomed a chalky white.

A few weeks later, when the construction came to an end and the scaffolding was removed, Archer stared up from the Glubs' garden at a house unlike any he'd ever seen. It was tall and skinny like all of the houses on Willow Street, but that's all it had in common.

"What is it?" asked Archer.

"I think it's French," said Mr. Glub. "Parisian, to be precise."

"Whatever it is, it's beautiful," said Mrs. Glub, who couldn't help but compare it to the garden they were standing in.

Archer was leaning against the garden wall so his mother wouldn't see him. Mrs. Helmsley was also staring out the windows at this most unusual home.

"Well," said Mr. Glub. "It might be beautiful, but I'll bet they don't have—" He stopped and searched the garden. "Where's my flamingo?"

Archer and Oliver slipped inside.

The movers arrived a few days later. Archer and Oliver

watched with the binoculars as furniture and boxes and all manner of odds and ends were carried throughout the house. It was quite the production. When the movers finished, the quiet of Willow Street was restored and with it, Archer's thoughts, which were now more dismal than ever. The boxes were gone. The journals were gone. His grandparents were gone. He had nothing except Helmsley House, which he would not be leaving for the foreseeable future.

If you've ever spent as much time in your house as Archer had, you might find yourself, as he did, growing pale and your spirits even paler. What hope did he have of restoring the Helmsley Golden Age from inside his house? What could he do in there that would make his grandparents proud? There was nothing he could do—nothing except feel very small while surrounded by their greatness. Archer shook his head. He wasn't like his grandfather. He was just a boy who fell asleep with his head inside a polar bear.

One week after the movers left, Archer and Oliver met on the rooftop as they did almost every night. Only this night was unlike other nights. In fact, this night would change everything in Archer's world. But Archer didn't know that yet. No, as he climbed the ladder to join Oliver, he was certain nothing in his world would ever change unless his grandparents returned.

✦ Icebergs Change Everything ✦

It was a cool, crisp evening. Archer licked his finger and held it above his head. "A slight south by southwest breeze?" he said.

"I think so," said Oliver, looking north by northeast.

The stars waited patiently for the sun to disappear behind the houses, then assumed their positions one by one, till the stage was set and the night began.

Archer was poking a stick in the gutter when he spotted a beetle crawling atop a leaf. He picked it up. He'd never seen one like this before. It was blue with yellow spots and looked quite special, but he wasn't interested. He flicked it down into the gardens. Oliver watched the beetle whiz by.

"I guess we'll find out if Mrs. Murkley really eats them," he said, hoping it would make Archer smile. It didn't.

Archer sat down next to him and dangled his legs over the edge.

"I used to think I was lucky to be a Helmsley," he said. "But it turned into a curse after the iceberg."

Archer was certain everything would be different had that not happened. But it had. And it seemed like a long time ago. More than two years now. That made it worse.

"They're not coming back," he admitted.

Archer had spent a considerable amount of time trying to figure out the life expectancy of an iceberg dweller and what he had concluded was troubling. He frequently ran the numbers, but the results were always the same. The main problem was fire.

"You couldn't survive without a fire," he said. "But you can't start one on an iceberg."

Oliver agreed, but after a moment, offered his own idea.

"Maybe they dug," he said.

"That doesn't make any sense. Where would you dig?"

"To the center of the iceberg," said Oliver with a shrug. "At least, that's what I would do."

Oliver had also given considerable thought to the situation. Oliver would dig. He would dig to the center of the iceberg because a small hole deep inside would be warm enough to keep him from freezing, but not be so warm as to melt the iceberg. And in the mornings, when the sun rose over the ocean, it would glisten through the thick walls of ice and that would be a beautiful sight to wake up to.

"The sun would warm the hole," he added with another shrug.

"Did you read that somewhere?" asked a befuddled Archer.

Oliver shook his head. "But I've been thinking about it ever since I saw the headline," he said. "I try to stay ahead of situations I might find myself in later on."

This was, in fact, a daily exercise for Oliver. Each night

he read his father's paper and tried to find solutions to the unfortunate situations other people found themselves in. Just in case.

Archer was confused. This was an Oliver he'd never seen before (mainly because Archer was too caught up in his own ideas to hear what Oliver might suggest). And what Oliver suggested was brilliant. But Oliver grew uncomfortable with Archer's staring and checked his forehead.

"Is something crawling on me?" he asked.

"We have to go to Antarctica," said Archer.

Oliver laughed, but Archer wasn't joking.

"You're serious?" said Oliver.

"Yes," said Archer.

"But that's impossible."

"It will be difficult." Archer corrected him. "But not impossible."

Oliver shook his head. "There are at least—at least three big problems with that. And the first is that even if you were successful—even if you somehow made it to Antarctica, you'd still probably die down there."

Archer leaned back on the roof and asked, "What else?"

Oliver blinked a few times. "That's not a big enough problem for you?" he said, then sighed and continued. "The second is that if you're not successful, if you get caught, you'll be shipped off to Raven Wood, which might be worse. The third is that you have no experience with anything of the sort. Antarctica is not an impulse destination."

He didn't like to do so, but Archer admitted he had no experience. He had no experience to do anything he wanted to do.

"But what if I found someone who did?" he said after a moment. "Someone who could help us? What if I went to Antarctica and found my grandparents? If I could make it happen, you would come with me, wouldn't you?"

Oliver didn't like the look in Archer's eye. This might be more serious than the library plans. Fortunately, Mr. Glub poked his head over the roof's edge.

"I had a feeling you'd be up here," he said. "And a good evening to you, Archer." Mr. Glub looked up at the stars. "A fine evening, isn't it? Makes me sorry to break you up, but Oliver wanted to help me organize the weeklies—unless he's changed his mind, of course."

Oliver hadn't changed his mind and was all too eager to escape. He said good-bye and climbed down the ladder. Archer disappeared down his ladder as well. He turned on his radio, left the balcony door open so he could hear it, and returned to the roof with his binoculars, which he pointed to the sky. He found the constellation

Orion—the great hunter—and for the first time in weeks, Archer smiled.

"Don't worry," he said. "We won't be stuck here much longer."

✦ CONSTELLATIONS ✦

Down in the gardens, the crickets exchanged moonlight pleasantries.

"Good evening," chirped one.

"Leave me alone," chirped another.

Up on the rooftop, Archer was still thinking about Antarctica. He did lack experience. He couldn't argue with that. But with the right help, with someone who did have experience, it wouldn't be impossible. He would need time to prepare and a ship to stow away on, and of course, a good escape plan because Oliver was right, the consequences of failing and getting caught would be great. But consequences don't matter when they're connected to something you *have* to do.

Archer continued to jump from constellation to constellation till he landed on the beginnings of one he did not recognize. He adjusted his binoculars. It wasn't a star. It was the garden light of the peculiar house on the opposite side of the garden.

"Your bedroom is upstairs," called the tall, well-groomed man, who had just turned on the garden light.

Archer watched the second-floor light flicker on, followed by the third-floor light, and finally, the top-floor light.

"It's the door on your left," said the tall, well-groomed man.

A girl entered the top-floor room carrying a suitcase. She was followed shortly by the tall, well-groomed man with more luggage. The girl went to the balcony door and stepped outside.

"Perhaps we should find you a room lower down," he said.

"This will be fine," the girl replied.

The man set the luggage down and left the room. The girl leaned against the railing and looked into the gardens. The south by southwest breeze changed directions and blew the music from Archer's bedroom to the girl's balcony. The girl spotted him. Archer quickly lowered his binoculars. She raised herself to the tips of her toes and, for a moment, stood perfectly still. Archer lifted his binoculars once more. The girl began spinning and it looked very pretty till she lost her balance and collapsed with a thud.

"*Sur la table, Adélaïde,*" the tall, well-groomed man called from the garden.

The girl picked herself up and stepped back inside. The top-floor light flickered off, followed by the third-floor light, and finally, the second-floor light.

Adélaïde? thought Archer. *What's an Adélaïde?*

✦ Rosewood Port & the Walrus ✦

Her name was Adélaïde. Adélaïde L. Belmont. Adélaïde is a French name.

"And how do you pronounce it?" asked the custom officer, looking up from her passport.

It took Adélaïde a moment to respond because she was enchanted by just how much this man resembled a walrus.

"Add—eh—lay—eed L. Bell—moan," she finally said. "The *t* is quiet."

"I think you mean it's *silent*," the walrus replied.

"No," she said. "Just quiet. You can sometimes hear it."

Adélaïde had a French name because Adélaïde was French, and Adélaïde was French because before she arrived in Rosewood Port, Adélaïde lived in France.

"And what brings you across the sea?" asked the officer.

Adélaïde bit her lip, tapped her fingers on the walrus's desk, and looked over her shoulder at her father, who was piling luggage onto a cart. She wasn't sure how to answer this question. She herself was surprised when her father made the announcement. That's not to say she was upset by it. On the contrary, Adélaïde was glad to leave France—but the reason?

"Ballet," she said, turning back to the walrus.

"So you're a ballerina?"

"Not anymore."

The officer raised an eyebrow. "Why not anymore?" he asked.

"Bread," she replied.

The officer raised a second eyebrow. "You're not a ballerina anymore because of *bread*?"

"Mostly just croissants," said Adélaïde.

At that, the walrus stood up and Adélaïde watched as he refilled his coffee, sharpened his pencil, and waddled back to his seat.

"I just want to make sure I have this straight," he said, looking over his notes. "You say you came across the sea for *ballet*, even though, thanks to *croissants*, you're no longer a ballerina. Is that correct?"

ROSEWOOD PORT

It was not completely correct and the order of events was a bit confused, but Adélaïde knew what she was doing so she smiled and nodded.

"Very well," the officer replied, having no idea what any of that was supposed to mean. He stamped her passport and handed it back to her. "Best of luck to you."

"*Merci, monsieur.*"

Adélaïde carried her suitcase outside. Her father hailed a taxicab and they piled their luggage into the trunk.

"Where to?" asked the cab driver.

"To three-seventy-six North Willow Street," Mr. Belmont said. He raised an invisible glass in the air. "And to a change of scenery."

Now before we continue, there's a chance some of you might be wondering many of the same things the walrus was.

Ballet? Bread? Quiet Ts?

It sounds like a bunch of nonsense, doesn't it? The truth is that it's not nonsense, but Adélaïde was a clever girl and while she didn't want to lie to an officer, she did want to confuse him because she didn't want to talk about it. So in order to answer these questions, it's best that we go back in time—back to the same time Archer opened his front door and discovered his grandparents had drifted out to sea atop an iceberg. When that happened, Adélaïde was nine and lived in France, in the north of Paris to be precise. And it's there that you now must go, whether by plane or boat or, *si tu préfères*, iceberg.

BON VOYAGE

✦ Part Two ✦

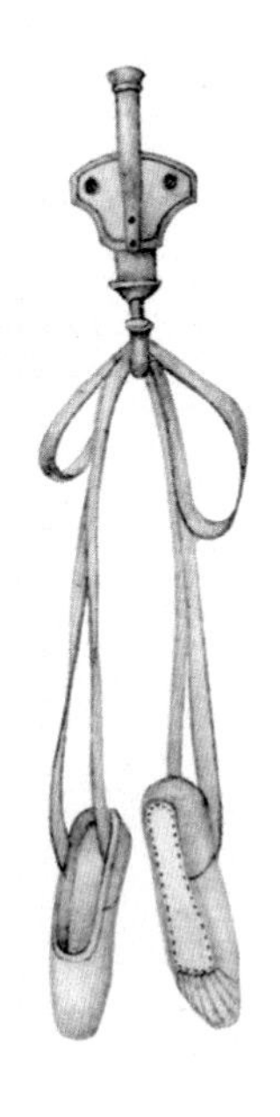

A GIRL FROM THE NORTH OF PARIS

CHAPTER

SEVEN

✦ A Girl in the North of Paris ✦

If you follow Rue de Girardon past the statue of the man who can walk through walls, continue down beyond the wooden windmill, slip through the narrow alleyway next to the yellow postbox, and follow along the bend, you'll arrive at Belmont Coffee & Café. This café was one of many owned by Adélaïde's father, a well-to-do coffee entrepreneur named François E. Belmont. And above this particular café was Adélaïde's home.

Adélaïde was a trifle small for a girl her age—perhaps even two or three trifles small. She was also a clever and kind and pleasantly sincere girl who by all means looked like any other perfectly normal nine-year-old girl. Yes, if you saw her on the street, you wouldn't think she was anything special or anything out of the ordinary, but that's where you'd be wrong. Adélaïde was someone special and *quite* out of the ordinary.

It begins with bread.

• Pathetic Croissants •

Adélaïde loved bread, all types of bread, and Paris is a very good city for the bread lover. Her personal favorite was the buttery and flaky croissant with chocolate baked inside. She could eat them all day long, for breakfast, lunch, and dinner (but her mother wouldn't hear of such nonsense). Fortunately, each morning at seven A.M., fresh bread was delivered to the Belmont café. And each morning at seven A.M., Adélaïde made her way down the stairs.

One morning, inside the café, Mr. Belmont was busy at work with an espresso machine and the barman, Amaury P. Guilbert, was eyeing a tray of croissants suspiciously. Adélaïde sat atop a barstool and watched him. Amaury was a gentle man, generously proportioned, and always wore a small cap, which Adélaïde thought made him look like a fishmonger. Or perhaps it was just his smell that did that. Either way, Adélaïde liked him.

"Is something wrong?" she asked.

Amaury placed the croissants in front of her.

"Do these look fresh to you?" he asked.

Adélaïde picked one up. A true bread connoisseur can instantly tell fresh bread from stale bread. "*It's all in the flakes*," Adélaïde will tell you. "*No flake? It's a fake.*" Adélaïde saw no flakes.

"I think they might be yesterday's," said Amaury.

"Or the day before yesterday's," agreed Adélaïde.

"Now tell me that's not delicious," said Mr. Belmont, turning from the espresso machine and placing a yellow cup in front of her. "It's a new espresso bean I'm selling. Take a sip—tell me what you think."

Adélaïde looked at the yellow cup. The yellow cup looked back at Adélaïde. For her own part, Adélaïde wasn't much of a coffee drinker. She preferred tea.

"That bread is stale again," said Amaury over his shoulder. "Third time this week."

Mr. Belmont wasn't listening.

"Go ahead, Adié," he said. "Tell me that's not exquisite."

Adélaïde took only a sip but that was enough. Her eyes sparked and her voice went fluty. "Exquisite," she squeaked, though she was thinking just the opposite. She now had espresso eyes—white all around with beady black dots at the centers.

Mr. Belmont picked up a croissant and took a bite.

"I think it's going to do very well and if we can"—he stopped and frowned at the sorry excuse for a pastry he just swallowed—"these are *awful*!"

"I just told you that," said Amaury. "Didn't I just say that, Adié?"

Adié shook her pinky. It was the best she could do.

"But that's the third time this week," said Mr. Belmont.

Amaury sighed. "Why do I even bother speaking to you?"

Mr. Belmont combed through the dismal pastries. "I think we have bad luck," he said. "Do we have bad luck?"

"No," said Amaury. "We have stale croissants."

Adélaïde blinked twice and slowly pushed the yellow cup away. She sorted through the bread, found two fresh croissants at the bottom, and said good-bye. On her way out, she passed a man who dropped a stack of papers next to the bar. She tilted her head sideways to read the headline.

LE PETIT JOURNAL

EXPLORERS ADRIFT IN ICY WATERS

"They had bad luck," Mr. Belmont said, and took another bite of the croissant, forgetting it was stale.

✦ Snails Become the Lady ✦

Adélaïde climbed the stairs back to the apartment. She stepped into the kitchen, set a wooden crate in front of the sink, and stood on top to fill a kettle with water. She then carried the kettle over to the stove, nudging the crate with her foot, and lit a burner to boil the water and make a cup of tea. She tapped her fingers against the counter, thinking the water never boiled fast enough when she had a croissant staring her in the face.

"I mustn't," she insisted, and turned from the pastry.

Her mother, Christine L. Belmont, was sitting at the kitchen table eating her breakfast.

"Who are you talking to?" she snipped, without looking up.

"Myself," Adélaïde replied.

"Then tell yourself to pipe down. I can't enjoy my breakfast with you running at the mouth all morning."

"But how can I tell myself to pipe down *and* pipe down at the same time?" she asked.

Mrs. Belmont did not respond. Instead, she bit into her toast with a crunch, and crumbs fell onto her otherwise spotless exterior. She lit a cigarette and vanished in a plume of smoke.

There are lots of different mothers in this world, but it's likely Mrs. Belmont would be at the bottom of almost everyone's list. Adélaïde didn't really know her mother because Mrs. Belmont was rarely to be seen. That was nothing terrible. Adélaïde preferred it, and if you had a mother like hers, you wouldn't be terribly upset if she was rarely around. Of course, sometimes it couldn't be avoided.

"Snails for the lady," said the waiter. "And what will your lovely daughter be eating this afternoon?"

"If you think she's so lovely, perhaps you'd like to take her," said Mrs. Belmont. "I can have the necessary paperwork to you in one hour."

The waiter blinked at her. Adélaïde shrugged.

"But how can you say that?" the waiter asked. "This is your daughter!"

Mrs. Belmont lit a cigarette. "Quite easily, monsieur, quite easily. I have a mole on my back. That mole belongs to me, but that does not mean I want it there."

Adélaïde made her tea, placed it on a tray with the croissants, and carefully walked up the stairs and out onto her rooftop. One croissant she gave to the pigeons waiting patiently for their breakfast, and the other she dipped into her tea and ate, perched on the roof's edge alongside the birds. When finished, she licked the buttery flakes from her fingertips and spun around to watch as the whole of Paris, stretching out as far she could see, came to life.

One of the birds cleared its throat.

"Do you think you were a pigeon in a previous life?" it asked.

"It's possible," Adélaïde replied. "But I doubt it."

"I think you were a croissant," said a second pigeon.

"If that's true," said the first, "there's a good chance we ate you."

"You must have," she said. "And then I became—"

"ADÉLAÏDE!" shouted Mrs. Belmont.

Adélaïde looked down. She couldn't see her mother, but was nearly certain she saw specks of spit reflecting the morning sunlight.

"I'm right *here*," she replied.

"I know where you are—that's why I'm yelling! Now stop frolicking with those birds and get yourself downstairs. Don't you keep Madame Lambert waiting one more minute!"

Adélaïde pulled the label off her tea bag, placed it in her pocket, and glanced at the pigeons as she loaded her tray.

"Eat her next time," she said. "She'll come back as a snail."

✦ The Paris Ballet Theater ✦

Mrs. Lambert was Adélaïde's tutor. Adélaïde was tutored at home, and the reason for this was ballet. Like most girls her age, Adélaïde wanted to be a ballerina. Unlike most girls her age, Adélaïde was a true prodigy of dance. At the age of six, she was admitted and enrolled into the Paris Ballet Theater, and because her time was spent in countless lessons, rehearsals, and performances, she couldn't attend normal school. Instead, she was tutored until one o'clock, after which she set off for the theater. It was a short walk, but Adélaïde enjoyed it. She packed her bag, slipped down the narrow alleyway next to the yellow postbox, continued past the wooden windmill, tapped the head of the man who could walk through walls, and followed the street to the theater.

It was an old, round building. She entered through a small door at the back and tried her best to slip past the front desk without Mr. Stanislas's notice and nearly succeeded but for a sudden and unexpected *hiccup*.

"*Ah*, Fräulein Adié."

Mr. Stanislas was the theater attendant and a most unpleasant man. His rusty words always left Adélaïde with a terrible aftertaste.

"Good afternoon," she replied, trying her best to smile.

Mr. Stanislas was not paid to exchange pleasantries so he rarely did. Instead, he clapped a messy stack of paper against his desk till the pages were uniformly aligned, all the while staring down his gravity-defiant nose at her.

"Have you been up on the roof feeding those filthy birds again?" he asked.

Adélaïde shrugged. "Maybe," she replied.

In fact, Adélaïde spent most of her breaks on the theater rooftop because Adélaïde was not terribly popular with the other young ballerinas. Mr. Stanislas stood up and leaned against the front of his desk with folded arms. Adélaïde stayed where she was.

"And how exactly does one *maybe* feed birds?" he asked. "I've seen people *feed* birds and I've seen people *not* feed birds, but I'm sorry to say I've never once seen someone *maybe* feed birds."

"They have to eat, too!" Adélaïde insisted.

"This is true, but not on my roof!" he barked. "And if you feed those creatures one more time, I'll send you up with the mop. I'll lose my job if the director sees that mess. Do we understand each other?"

They didn't, but Adélaïde nodded and continued down the hall, rubbing her tongue against the roof of her mouth to rid herself of that terrible taste. The theater halls were littered with young ballerinas, stretching and warming up. They whispered and giggled as Adélaïde passed. Her room was number seventeen. She stepped inside to change.

• Ballet of Adélaïde L. Belmont •

It was not long before Adélaïde rose above the other *petits rats* (as the young ballerinas are called at the Paris Ballet Theater) to the top of her class. Her exceptional talent was well noted by the instructors. But not everything was like bread with chocolate baked inside. There were plenty of snails served along, too. The other *petits rats* were jealous of the fuss and attention paid to Adélaïde.

"I think she's cheating."

"Is that even possible?"

"She looks more like a fish flopping around, if you ask me."

"That doesn't matter. Mr. Ravel thinks she's better than us."

"Not just Mr. Ravel. *She* thinks she's better than us."

While none of this was true, it didn't matter. The *petits rats* would join hands and dance in circles around her singing:

We hope that you, Miss Pirouette,
Will see a day you won't forget
A change in your nice silhouette
Just like the young queen, Antoinette!

Adélaïde made her solo debut at the age of eight. It was a young persons' concert, which meant tickets were sold at half price and even then, many seats were left empty. But that didn't matter to Adélaïde.

The performance began at eight, so she told her father to be there at seven, knowing even then he would still be late.

"To the Paris Ballet Theater, and step on it!" shouted Mr. Belmont as he jumped into a taxi.

He dashed up theater steps and straight into the outstretched hands of Mr. Stanislas.

"I'm sorry, but I can't let you in," Mr. Stanislas said.

"But that's my daughter in there," Mr. Belmont replied.

Mr. Stanislas peered at the stage through a glass window in the door.

"The Fräulein?" he asked.

Mr. Belmont raised an eyebrow. "If that's what you call her."

"Well, rules are rules," said Mr. Stanislas with a sickly grin. "I'm not supposed to allow anyone in once the performance has begun."

Mr. Belmont was silent a moment, then said, "Would you mind getting me a glass of water, at least? I just ran the entire way here."

Mr. Stanislas sniveled. Mr. Belmont insisted.

"Wait here," Mr. Stanislas said, slithering from his post.

Once he was out of sight, Mr. Belmont slipped inside.

✦

Often years pass from one to the next and blend without distinction. But every once in a while, you'll have a year that sticks out. It can be a good thing or a bad thing that makes it so. For Adélaïde, it was her ninth year that stuck out and the reason for this was a bad thing. It all began early one morning with the baking of bread.

• The Bakery Truck & the Lamppost •

A baker of bread must wake up early in the morning and a baker of bread must spend those early morning hours shoveling fresh dough in and out of hot ovens. It's a difficult life but a necessary one as this is the only way the rest of us can enjoy fresh bread. The bread supplier for Belmont Coffee & Café was a baker named Christoph, and Christoph was good at what he did. The only problem was Christoph always woke up late and often didn't have time to make fresh bread. As a result, he sold yesterday's bread and sometimes, the day-before-yesterday's bread.

"Stale again," said Amaury.

"Not a flake in sight," said Adélaïde.

Mr. Belmont picked up the phone. "...I understand, Christoph, but if you swindle me one more time with these stale croissants, I will find someone else."

✦

With the looming threat of losing his largest client, Christoph had no choice. He set three alarm clocks next to his bed and started waking up early every single morning to make fresh bread. Eventually, this began to have an odd effect on him. Christoph started seeing things that weren't really there, and seeing things that aren't really there has gotten lots of people into lots of trouble.

Early one morning, after spending hours shoveling dough into ovens, Christoph and his partner, Nicolas, loaded their bread truck and set off for the Belmont Coffee & Café. Somewhere in transit, his mind began to play tricks on him. Christoph glanced into his side view mirror and thought he saw a single pigeon chasing the truck. But pigeons don't chase trucks, so Christoph shrugged it off. A moment later, he thought he spotted five more. He turned to Nicolas.

"Did you see . . ."

"See what?" asked Nicolas.

"Maybe I'm just . . ."

"Just what?"

Christoph shook his head. "Never mind," he said.

Nicolas raised an eyebrow and the volume on the radio. As Nicolas did this, Christoph was quite certain he spotted no fewer than thirty-seven birds in hot pursuit. No, he couldn't be crazy! He saw them as clearly as you now see this book.

"We're being hunted!" Christoph shouted.

"Hunted by who?" asked Nicolas calmly.

"Not *who*. Pigeons!"

Nicolas peered into his side view mirror. He blinked twice and then once more. The illusive birds did not appear.

"You haven't been at the crepes and cider again, have you?" he asked with concern.

Christoph adamantly denied the charge. "It's the bread! They want my bread!" He slammed on the accelerator and went barreling down the street. Nicolas tightened his seat belt.

In truth, the only pigeons to be found were the ones perched atop Adélaïde's rooftop waiting for her and, more importantly, their breakfast. But the pigeons weren't the only ones waiting for their breakfast. The night before, Adélaïde had left the rooftop door open a crack and her cat Napoleon had gone to investigate after seeing the morning sunlight slanting down the stairs. He stepped out onto the rooftop and into a delicious situation.

Perched along the edge were countless pigeons, all still half asleep. Napoleon crouched low, trying to decide which one he should eat first. After making his decision, he moved in for the kill. Quick as a whip, the cat pounced. Pigeons flew everywhere, swooping and swarming this way and that. Napoleon was overwhelmed. He leaped into the air to catch one, but in the chaos, caught nothing. The birds regrouped. They swooped clean over the roof's edge and down into the streets below.

The foolish creatures were in such a panic that they flew headlong into the bakery truck now barreling down the street. The pigeons bounced lifelessly off the windshield and plopped onto people who wished they'd stayed in bed.

Nicolas shrieked.

"I told you!" shouted Christoph. He released the steering wheel and covered his face. The truck swerved left and right and out of control.

It was seven A.M. Adélaïde stepped out her front door. The bakery truck screeched sideways down the street. The tires were about to explode. Pigeons swarmed. People shouted. Croissants rolled. Everywhere were feathers. Adélaïde stared with espresso eyes. *These sorts of things don't happen!*

The bakery truck smashed sideways into a lamppost and all fell silent. But the impact dislodged the lamppost from the sidewalk. The lamppost wavered. An eerie moan of metal sounded when, a moment later, the lamppost fell. Adélaïde was too shocked to move in time.

• The Queen of Farce •

"I'm going away for a short while," Mr. Belmont announced one afternoon.

Two years had passed since the bakery truck incident, and Adélaïde was now nearly eleven. It had been a foggy two years for her, and she emerged from that fog with a wooden leg. She was no longer enrolled at the Paris Ballet Theater but was still tutored at home. She wasn't sure what to think about all this so she didn't. She didn't want to talk about it, either. No matter where she went, people would stare. (The polite ones would pretend they didn't notice.) So Adélaïde stayed home. And while her father was away, busied herself with Amaury in the café.

One afternoon she was sitting at the bar playing cards with Amaury when a short, disgruntled-looking man approached. He placed his order and proceeded to stare most impolitely at her leg.

"You pick up a bad penny or something?" he asked.

Adélaïde stared at Amaury over her cards. He grinned and leaned against the bar. "You want to tell him or should I?"

"I think it's best if you tell him," she replied, choosing a card.

Amaury glanced at the disgruntled man.

"What do you know about crocodiles?" he asked.

"*Crocodiles?*" the man repeated.

Adélaïde nodded. "Chewed it clean off," she said, and played her card.

Amaury placed one atop hers. "Nasty creatures, they are," he said.

"Horrible teeth," she added.

Amaury and Adélaïde laughed as the disgruntled man left without his coffee. Later that day, Amaury went to the opposite side of Paris to check in on another Belmont café. Adélaïde made a cup of tea and slipped into the back of the shop. She wove through a mountain of boxes labeled "Belmont Coffee" and rogue beans littered across the floor. Against a shelf was a table struggling to support a large ham radio. It looked like something the military would use, but it was only Amaury who used it. The radio was a hobby of his, and he spent most of his breaks sitting before it. The chair

BELMONT
COFFEE
BELMON
COFFEE

squeaked as Adélaïde sat down and took a sip of tea. The machine looked complicated, but she clicked the on switch and twisted the knobs (as she'd seen Amaury do countless times) saying "*Bonjour*" into the microphone as she did.

"*Brochure?*" returned the static voice of a boy.

Adélaïde leaned forward. "*Oui. Bonjour!*" she replied.

"*Free brochure?*"

"Oui! Bonjour," said Adélaïde, thinking this boy not too bright for simply repeating what she said.

"*Thanks, but I'm not interested in a free brochure.*"

At this, Adélaïde realized the boy was speaking English. She quickly said "Hello" but the connection was lost.

• A Change of Scenery •

Mr. Belmont returned home two months later and made a second announcement. "We're moving across the sea."

As a general rule, almost anyone who lives in Paris never wants to leave it. But as with most rules, there are a few exceptions. Mr. Belmont was one such exception. He thought Adélaïde needed a change of scenery. His search for a new home led him across the sea to the city of Rosewood, where he purchased house number 376 on North Willow Street. And to give his family a little taste of home, he decided to have it remodeled in a proper Parisian fashion. But when the construction was complete and moving day arrived, Mrs. Belmont was nowhere to be found. Mrs. Belmont was not an exception to the rule. She had no desire to leave her beloved city. So she didn't.

For her own part, Adélaïde was glad to leave. She didn't like living in the shadow of the Paris Ballet Theater. She packed the last of her belongings into her suitcase and followed her father to the docks. They walked up a gangplank and stepped onto an ocean liner.

After a few days of sea breezes, Adélaïde saw seagulls and then she saw land. She disembarked, made her way through Rosewood Port, and stepped outside. There was a pleasant breeze at her back and she was glad to be somewhere new.

She looked out at the twisting streets leading away from the port. The city wasn't half as big as Paris but seemed just as old. There was the beginning of a canal lined with tall buildings and she wanted to take a closer look, but her father called to her. They piled their luggage into a taxi and hopped inside.

"Where to?" asked the cab driver.

"To three-seventy-six North Willow Street," Mr. Belmont said. He raised an invisible glass in the air. "And to a change of scenery."

7

CHAPTER

EIGHT

⬩ Goldfinch Spy ⬩

Adélaïde was sitting on her balcony eating her breakfast (tea and croissant) and reading a book (*Perils for Pearls*). But she read the same sentence three times because she couldn't shake the feeling that she was being watched. This was nothing new, of course. But ever since she had moved to North Willow Street two weeks ago, Adélaïde felt it especially so. She lowered her book and saw a goldfinch perched on the railing. It was staring at her.

It's the bird, she thought. *That bird has been watching me.*

She kicked her wooden leg at the winged creature until it reluctantly flew off the ledge.

Down below, Napoleon the cat was lurking atop the garden walls in a morning stupor when he spotted Mrs. Murkley asleep in a garden chair. Not far away, also atop the walls, the non-nocturnal opossum looked up as the goldfinch swooped across the gardens and landed on a windowsill of house number 375. Inside that window, Archer lowered his binoculars.

"What did you find out?" he asked.

The goldfinch wouldn't say a word till Archer gave it some toast. He broke off the crust and tossed it onto the sill, but the bird wanted the good stuff so Archer threw everything he had. The bird greedily pecked away.

"Well?" asked Archer after a moment.

The bird ignored him.

"Who are you talking to?" said Oliver, who was lying on the floor of Archer's room. He turned his head toward the bed. "And why is there an eyeball under your bed?"

Archer glanced over his shoulder. He'd forgotten about his glass eye. "I'm not talking to anyone," he replied and, turning back to the goldfinch, pressed for information.

The bird finally spoke between pecks.

"I've flown—around the block—once or twice—in my life—but—*CAW*—excuse me. But never, not once, have I seen someone like that. She has a wooden leg!"

Yes, Archer could see that. "But why?" he asked.

"I've not the slightest idea," the bird replied.

Archer was annoyed he'd given up his toast for this. He

swatted the plate at the goldfinch but accidentally let the plate go. Both the bird and the plate crashed to the garden floor. Adélaïde lowered her book. Mrs. Murkley jumped to her feet, fists at the ready. Oliver ran to the window.

"Why'd you kill it?" he asked, staring down at the stunned bird.

"I didn't mean to," said Archer, feeling terrible and quickly leaning farther out the window. "But I don't think it's dead."

It wasn't. Not yet. But Napoleon the cat was quicker than the non-nocturnal opossum.

Oliver sighed. "I guess that's that."

Mrs. Helmsley dashed into the gardens to inspect the shattered plate and three golden feathers. She turned up toward Archer's window just as Archer and Oliver ducked inside. Archer went to his bed. Oliver stayed at the window to watch Adélaïde, who was back to reading her book.

"I wonder what she'd look like with two legs," he said.

"Do you think it would make any difference?"

"Probably not."

Archer dug beneath his pillow and found his notebook. "Never mind her," he said. "We have other things to worry about."

Two weeks had passed since their conversation on the rooftop, and Archer was still set on Antarctica despite

Oliver's incessant reminder that he would need someone with experience if he had the slightest hope of doing such a thing. Archer knew this was true. But he also knew there was research he could do on his own—research that required the Button Factory library. Fortunately, school began in three days. But when school did start, Archer was distracted.

• Thimbleton & Murkley •

On the first day of school, Adélaïde arrived at the Button Factory early to meet with Mrs. Thimbleton, the head of school, who looked just as a Thimbleton should. After her welcome, she asked Adélaïde a series of questions while writing a note.

"I would like you to meet with Miss Whitewood after class," she said. "I'll let her know you're coming. She'll give you a tour of our school and help with anything you might need."

Mrs. Thimbleton pointed her pen at Adélaïde's leg. "You'll need assistance getting around, yes?"

Adélaïde leaned back in the chair and shook her head, tired of everyone assuming she needed help.

"I'll be fine," she replied.

"Very well," said Mrs. Thimbleton. She finished her note

and was about to hand it to Adélaïde when she froze, her eyes fixed on something just beyond the girl's head. Adélaïde turned and found a brutish woman clogging the doorway. Adélaïde knew this woman. Or at least, she'd seen her in the Willow Street gardens.

"Margery!" Mrs. Thimbleton cried. "How delightful it is to see you again!"

"Of course it's *delightful* to see me," Mrs. Murkley replied. "Let's not waste time stating the obvious, my dear Mrs. Thimbleton. And please, call me *Mrs. Murkley*."

Mrs. Thimbleton smiled. "Yes, well, we were all terribly upset to hear what happened at Raven Wood, of course. But the past is the past, and we mustn't harp on it. Raven Wood's loss is the Willow Academy's gain. Yes, our students are most fortunate you accepted my offer."

"Of course they are," said Mrs. Murkley. "Honestly, it's a wonder you accomplish anything during the day."

"It just so happens," said the rather proud and sunny Mrs. Thimbleton, "that I've just finished organizing a special welcome for the students this year. Now if you'll come sit down and stop giving Adélaïde here the wrong impression with all your lurking in doorways, I'll tell you about it so you can surprise your class first thing this morning."

Mrs. Thimbleton gave Adélaïde the note. Adélaïde thanked her and circumnavigated Mrs. Murkley, doubting the brutish woman saw her at all because she nearly slammed the door on her good leg.

It was still early and there was time before class, so Adélaïde decided to wander the halls. The Button Factory was a unique place, but its seemingly endless pale yellow corridors dotted with countless windows felt uncomfortably familiar to her. After getting lost a number of times, she poked her head into a students' room. There was one for each grade, and she thought it looked comfortable. She walked past the armchairs and couches and sat in a window seat overlooking a vast unkempt courtyard with a crumbling fountain at the center. She stayed there awhile, watching as tiny dots of students made their way along winding paths. In groups of two and three, students began trickling into the room. They sat together on couches, but no one noticed the girl in the window.

Against the far wall were two lavatory doors. Adélaïde left the window and stepped inside the girls' room to tighten her leg. Just as she finished, Alice P. Suggins entered.

• Crocodile in Denial •

Adélaïde stood before a long row of sinks pretending not to notice the girl who was now glaring at her.

"That's an ugly sock," said Alice.

"It's not a sock," she replied. "It's a wooden leg."

Alice (who was a girl with the grace of a swan yet the killer instincts of a hawk) swooped in to get a closer look.

"What happened to you?" Alice asked.

Adélaïde met the girl's eyes. "A crocodile," she replied, and turned back to the sink to wash her hands.

Alice didn't buy it. "Where would you have seen a crocodile?" she said with her nose to the air. "There are no *crocodiles* in *Rosewood*."

The first thing that popped into Adélaïde's head was *the Nile, as a matter of fact* and that's what she said. "I'm not from Rosewood," she added. "Can't you tell from my accent?"

Alice did notice the accent. "*The Nile?*" she repeated.

"Yes, the Nile is filled with crocodiles."

Adélaïde dried her hands and left the girls' lavatory, hoping that would put an end to it. It didn't. Alice couldn't keep such a story to herself. A few hallway whispers later, Adélaïde's tiny thread of misinformation was woven into a magnificent tapestry depicting a tale of adventure and mischance and woe.

"She was traveling across Egypt," said Charlie H. Brimble. "In a hot air balloon."

"And she wanted to photograph the Nile," said Molly S. Mellings. "But she leaned too far and fell in."

"She was lucky enough to survive," said Alice P. Suggins. "But a crocodile ripped her leg clean off."

MEMBER OF THE ROSEWOOD PUBLIC LIBRARY

WILLOW ACADEMY LIBRARY

• BOOK REQUEST CARD •

REQUEST NO. 37954

Miss Whitewood,

Would you please find a book on crocodiles? Where they live and what they eat. Thanks.

Archer Helmsley

Archer tapped the request card against the second-floor book request station while looking over his shoulder at Oliver.

"Are you sure?" he asked.

Oliver wasn't. "But that's what everyone is saying. You've seen her leg. That's not normal."

It certainly wasn't. Archer put the request card into a container and the container into the tube to the library. A healthy dose of jealousy enveloped him as they hurried down the corridors to class.

"What kind of person falls out of a hot air balloon in the desert?" he asked.

"A reckless one," said Oliver.

"No," said Archer. "One like my grandparents. They survived a desert plane crash. I've never survived anything."

"That's a good thing," said Oliver.

Archer disagreed.

"Well, your head was inside the jaws of a polar bear. That's something."

"It might be," said Archer. "If the polar bear wasn't dead."

Archer and Oliver found their class and took two seats at the back of the room. Hearing all of the students whispering about Adélaïde made Archer feel worse. It's an odd thing to be jealous of a girl whose leg was eaten by a crocodile. Few people would be jealous of that. But Archer was few people. And it wasn't so much the loss of a limb as it was the entire story. Archer knew a great many people were able to do a great many things he couldn't—*but my own neighbor? Living just across the gardens?*

"It can't be true," Archer said.

Oliver opened his mouth to reply, but stopped. The room fell silent. Archer spun around. The crocodile girl was standing in the doorway.

You might think Adélaïde would be nervous because she was in a new country and she'd never attended a real school before, but Adélaïde was never a casualty of stage fright. Still, as she walked past the stares and sniggers of the other students to take her seat in the final desk of the final row, she wished she could blend in better.

"She doesn't look like she's done such things," Archer whispered.

"That means it's probably true," said Oliver. "My father says I should never trust someone who looks the part."

Adélaïde sat quietly staring out the window, ignoring the whispers that began once more. She didn't have to ignore them for long, because a minute later the door flew open and knocked against the blackboard with a force strong enough to blow every last whisper out the open windows. Archer's heart took a hit with the blackboard. This wasn't the first time he'd seen a door open like that.

CHAPTER
NINE

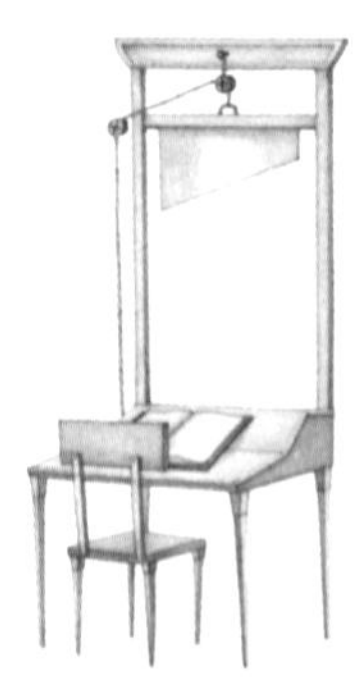

• Arctic-Related Accidents •

Mrs. Murkley marched across the room without acknowledging a single student. She plopped her bag and a stack of papers on the desk and proceeded to stare out the window for a few moments. The students exchanged glances. Everyone seemed to be thinking the same thing:

Did she see us? thought Charlie H. Brimble.
Is she blind? thought Molly S. Mellings.
She needs a new dress, thought Alice P. Suggins.

The other students knew nothing about their new teacher. Archer did. And he couldn't believe his luck, if luck is the right word. He had managed to avoid being seen by Mrs. Murkley all summer long. Now she stood before him, in all her glory, and he was certain she would do a number on him. He lowered his head to the desk behind a well-fed boy named Digby Fig.

Mrs. Murkley left the window to assume her position in front of the class. She studied the young faces looking back at her and appeared to dissect them, one by one. After this preliminary once-over, she began.

"My name is Mrs. Murkley," she announced without ceremony. "And it's quite clear in looking at all of you that your feeble Mrs. Thimbleton has been running a rather loose ship. This changes now."

Before she could continue, Alice raised her hand. Mrs. Murkley twisted her head in the girl's direction.

"A problem already?" she asked.

Alice shook her brightly beaming head from side to side. "First of all," she said. "I wanted to say that I love your dress. I also wanted to be the first to welcome you to our school. My name is Alice and I will be glad to assist with anything you might need."

Mrs. Murkley's smile was not one to warm the cockles of your heart.

"A kind gesture, my dear Alice," she replied. "And I have one for you as well. I shall place you at the very *top* of my list."

Mrs

Alice allowed herself a proud smile. "Thank you," she replied.

Mrs. Murkley's laugh didn't warm the cockles either. "And why, may I ask, are you smiling?" she snorted.

"Because—" Alice hesitated, "because it's good to be on top."

"Yes, I'm sure that's the case elsewhere in this school," said Mrs. Murkley. "But I can assure you that in here, it's the very last place you'll want to be. Now are you quite finished with your little routine?"

Alice blushed. "What routine?" she asked quietly.

Mrs. Murkley soured. "*Honestly*, Alice! You love my dress, do you?" She turned to the rest of the class. "I would like everyone to take good note of this. Our dear Alice here is a perfect example of why one mustn't spend too much time in the sunlight. Now put your elixirs away. I'm not buying anything. And pipe down. I don't want to hear another word from you."

The students shifted in their seats. For reasons Archer couldn't figure out, Charlie Brimble threw up his hand.

"What's he doing?" whispered Archer.

"Committing suicide," whispered Oliver.

Mrs. Murkley groaned. "Can't I get two words out before you all start laying your issues at my feet?"

Charlie lowered his hand a little.

"Come now, string bean," Mrs. Murkley continued. "Tell us your problem. Clothes can't find enough hip or shoulder to grab on to? Whatever it is, I can't promise results, but I'll roll up the sleeves and try my best."

With the entire class and Mrs. Murkley now glaring at him, Charlie's thoughts bounced around like an egg being hard-boiled.

"I—*uh*, I just—" he tried.

Mrs. Murkley shook her head. "This place is far worse than I thought," she said. "I've seen tree stumps with greater cognition."

She folded her arms and tapped her foot while waiting for Charlie to say something, but it's awfully difficult to think once your thoughts have been hard-boiled. All Charlie managed was, "Never mind."

Mrs. Murkley grinned. "*Very good,*" she chirped. "I sense improvement in you already. Still, let's put you in slot number two on my list so Alice won't feel alone. Now where was I?" Mrs. Murkley looked out at the sea of students and caught sight of Archer.

Archer still had his head lowered to his desk, and while some adults might struggle to tell the difference between a boy and plank of a wood, Mrs. Murkley was a professional and well versed in the defining aspects of each. "*It's all in the grain,"* she'll tell you. *"A boy will have countless more knots than a plank of wood."*

Something peculiar happened when Mrs. Murkley saw him. He assumed she would be furious. He'd sent her to the hospital, after all. The strange thing was, she didn't look angry. Not in the least. It was just the opposite, in fact. She appeared downright gleeful, as though she might burst at the seams and he would have to duck as chunks of Murkley soared over his head. Archer's palms grew sweaty.

"*Alfred!*" she cried. "*Oh yes!* I did so very much hope to see you in my class. I take back what I said about Mrs. Thimbleton. She's a clever lady, that one. Thought you did away with me, did you?"

The students twisted their necks to stare at Archer.

> "And it goes without saying," Mrs. Helmsley had said just before Archer left the house that morning. "That if you see Mrs. Murkley, you will apologize."

While engaging this woman a second time was the last thing Archer wanted to do, he took a deep breath, raised his head, and tried his best to explain the accident.

"*Accident?*" repeated Mrs. Murkley. "You want me to believe it was an *accident*? That's rich, my dear. Chocolate fudge, that is. So you *accidentally* fell asleep with your head inside a polar bear's mouth? And you *accidentally* rolled a glass eye from that mouth. *I see*. And then you *accidentally* tried to explode my heart?"

The students exchanged grins. They were fascinated. Mrs. Murkley turned to them.

"Tell me," she said, "has anyone here *accidentally* fallen asleep with their head inside a polar bear?"

Not a single hand went up.

"I wouldn't think so," said Mrs. Murkley. She clasped her hands and flashed Archer a poisonous smile. "But perhaps you're right, Alfred. Perhaps the whole ordeal *was* an accident, as you say. Yes, your family *does* have a rather peculiar history of Arctic-related accidents, don't they?"

Archer bit his tongue and turned a light mauve, sorry he'd opened his mouth. Oliver began poking him in the back. He knew what it meant. It meant, *Don't do something foolish and get yourself thrown out a window or shipped off to Raven Wood*. But as Mrs. Murkley took a few steps in their direction, the poking stopped.

"Yes, perhaps it was an accident," Mrs. Murkley continued. "But today is a new day. Today we put this *accidental* lifestyle of yours up on the shelf. Today we replace it with a *purposeful* existence. That's the task I see before me. That's why I'm here.

That's what brought me to your doorstep. There's hope for you yet, my dear boy, and I must try my best, for we should all *very much hate* to see you go the way of the iceberg like those *loons*."

Archer's toes curled and he bubbled with anger.

"They're not loons," he said quietly, behind clenched teeth.

"What's that?" asked Mrs. Murkley.

"I said they're not *loons*."

"But of course they are, my dear. Even *you* must see that." She addressed the class once more. "Has anyone here had a family member float out to sea atop an iceberg?"

No one raised a hand. Mrs. Murkley gave a thoughtful nod.

"Why does this not surprise me?" she asked. "Ah yes, because *normal* people don't float out to sea atop icebergs, do they?"

"Normal people don't shout at the moonlight!" cried Oliver.

At least, that's what Oliver thought about doing. In truth, Oliver was looking the opposite way, trying his best to disassociate himself from Archer. Across the room, Adélaïde watched in amazement.

• Heads Where Heads Ought Not Be •

Adélaïde was no stranger to nastiness. Her mother, you'll remember, was most unpleasant, and she could sometimes still taste Mr. Stanislas's rusty words, and of course there were the attacks from the *petits rats*. But Mrs. Murkley was not a *petit rat*. Mrs. Murkley was a Mouse King. At least, that's how the ballerina saw it. And while she knew nothing of this Alfred or his polar bear or the iceberg, she didn't like what she was seeing, so before Mrs. Murkley could say another word, Adélaïde cleared her throat and said, "*Pardon*, Mrs. Murk-*lay*."

Mrs. Murkley spun around.

"Who called out like that?" she snapped.

Adélaïde raised her hand. Jaws dropped all around and though no one said a word, they were all thinking the same thing.

It's the crocodile girl!

Mrs. Murkley left Archer's desk, marched across the room, and raised herself to her full height. Adélaïde, already a trifle small for a girl her age, looked even smaller beneath the behemoth, but she stared back without hesitation. Mrs. Murkley's ears went pink. This one would be trouble.

"First of all," she said. "The name is Murk-*ley*, not Murk-*lay*. Second of all, there are rules in this classroom, my dear. I will not tolerate you calling out willy-nilly like this."

"I'm sorry," said Adélaïde. "This is my first day in a real school."

Mrs. Murkley blinked and tilted her head. "What do you mean this is your *first* day in a *real* school?"

"I lived in France," Adélaïde replied. "I wasn't able to attend school."

"Are there no schools in France?"

"There are plenty," said Adélaïde. "But I was tutored."

"Too troubled to attend a proper institution, no doubt," Mrs. Murkley snipped at the same moment she noticed Adélaïde's leg. "*Very* troubled, I see. Where's your other leg? Are you trying to make me look extravagant for going about on two?"

Adélaïde shook her head while suppressing a smile.

"No, Mrs. Murkley," she replied. "I don't think you're extravagant."

A few brave students giggled. Mrs. Murkley's pink ears drained into her face and deepened in hue. She couldn't tell if this girl was being coy. But that didn't matter. Mrs. Murkley was clearly losing her patience.

"I knew you were going to be trouble," she snapped. "Yes, the very moment I introduced myself and saw you staring out that window with your head up in the clouds."

Mrs. Murkley lowered a hand to Adélaïde's desk and positioned her head so close that Adélaïde could count her nose hairs.

"From now on, you'll keep your mouth *shut* and that little head of yours inside this classroom where it belongs!"

Adélaïde slowly turned and gazed out the window. "But don't you think the clouds are very pretty?" she asked.

This small act of defiance had a tremendous effect on Mrs. Murkley. Her giant head flushed a brilliant red and her nostrils flared. She looked like she might blow a gasket. The other students tried their best to back away while still remaining in their seats.

"Gorgeous!" Mrs. Murkley shouted. "But if I instruct you to keep your head inside this classroom, you'll do well to obey!"

"In France," said Adélaïde, facing Mrs. Murkley once more,"they tell us to be mindful with those who dictate head placement because these could be the same people who someday tell you to stick it in a guillotine."

"You'll stick your head where I tell you to stick it!" Mrs. Murkley demanded. "In a guillotine or wherever! If you don't, there *will* be consequences!"

Adélaïde nodded. "*But*," she said slowly, "what consequences would be worse than sticking my head in a guillotine?"

Mrs. Murkley sputtered and turned a color that was difficult to describe. Her lips were tight and her eyes were slits and her heart beat wildly. For Mrs. Murkley, a wildly beating heart was never a good thing. Adélaïde sensed a problem.

"Are you all right?" she asked.

Mrs. Murkley pointed a shaky finger at her. "Girls who are missing legs are in no position to question the wellness of others!" she shouted, her voice cracking.

But that was the end of it. Mrs. Murkley tramped to the front of the classroom and stood silently facing the blackboard. The students, who were still fixated on Adélaïde, quickly spun around when they heard Mrs. Murkley sit down.

It's always troubling for a woman like Mrs. Murkley when someone so much smaller gains the upper hand. It upsets the natural order of things. What's worse was Adélaïde did so with no effort.

The room was perfectly silent while Mrs. Murkley tried to regain her composure. When she finally stood up once more, her voice remained shaky.

"As this is the first day of school," she said, "I think it best to be lenient, as I trust you've all observed." She lifted the stack of papers from her desk. "Now for reasons I won't pretend to understand, your head of school saw fit to send each class to the Rosewood Museum for a day of—a day of"—she looked down and read, "*a day of on-site learning with lots of good cheer, to welcome you all to a lovely new year."*

The entire class giggled, but a glance from Mrs. Murkley was enough to silence them all. She dropped a pile on the first desk of each row and the students passed them back.

THE WILLOW ACADEMY

ROSEWOOD MUSEUM

A day of on-site learning with lots of good cheer
To welcome you all to a lovely new year

This year, each class will spend a day at the Rosewood Museum. It is our sincere hope that this will inspire much productivity for the year. We are also excited to announce that the museum has partnered with the Rosewood Zoo and each class will have a unique experience.

As your basics teacher is: Mrs. Murkley, you will go to the museum on: Monday, the 6th of October. In order to attend, please have your parents sign this slip and return it to your basics teacher.

____
Signature

____
Signature

I wish you all the best this year.

Sincerely,

Mrs. Thimbleton

Mrs. Thimbleton

Willow Academy Head of School

"Make no mistake," Mrs. Murkley continued. "I do not believe in such frivolity and it will end with this trip. If your parents don't sign these slips, such frivolity ends *now*."

She grabbed her bag and left the room before the morning break bell sounded. The students stared at one another as the air came back into the room.

"What just happened?" Charlie asked.

"This is going to be a long year," Alice said to Molly as they made for the door. Charlie ran after them.

Archer was studying Adélaïde, but quickly turned away when she smiled at him.

"I have to go to the bathroom," he said, and stood up.

"Good idea," said Oliver, following him out. "I think I might throw up, too."

CHAPTER TEN

✦ Crocodile Indigestion ✦

An entire year lay ahead—an entire year with Mrs. Murkley. That was enough to send almost everyone running to DuttonLick's when the final bell rang to drown their sorrows in something sweet. That's what Oliver wanted to do, but Archer was going to the library so he followed. Judging from their expressions, you'd think it was Oliver, not Archer, who was on the top of Mrs. Murkley's list.

"Strictly speaking," said Oliver. "Do you think it's legal allowing someone like her to teach? She's not stable."

Archer was only half listening. He bent down to pick up a button, then pushed through the library doors. Miss Whitewood greeted them warmly from behind her desk.

"I won't pretend to know what this is about," she said. "But here's a book that might help you."

She set the book on the counter and returned to her paperwork. Archer thanked her and turned to leave, but Oliver hesitated. He leaned against her desk and said, "Can I ask you a question, Miss Whitewood?"

"You just did," Miss Whitewood replied, still reviewing a form. "But you may ask another if you wish."

"Thanks," said Oliver. "I was just curious to know if you've met the new teacher, Mrs. Murkley?"

Miss Whitewood's pen froze. "I've known her for some time," she said. "Why do you ask? Is she one of your teachers?"

Archer and Oliver nodded. Miss Whitewood nodded back and lowered her voice. "You *must* stay out of trouble," she warned. "She has no tolerance for disobedience. None of any kind. You must keep to her good side."

"But she only has one side," said Oliver. "And it's not a good one."

"Just keep your head down. You'll be fine."

They left Miss Whitewood's desk.

"What do you think it means to be on her list?" Oliver asked.

"She can't kill us," Archer said. He wasn't half as worried about Mrs. Murkley as Oliver was.

"Doesn't mean she won't try," Oliver mumbled.

Alice and Charlie were walking out of the reading room as Archer and Oliver entered.

"Steer clear of those icebergs," they said, laughing.

Archer grumbled and took a seat. Oliver did the same, watching Charlie. "He really doesn't have much hip or shoulder for his clothes to hold on to," he said. "Mrs. Murkley was right about that."

Archer gave him a little smile and opened the book.

DIETARY HABITS OF CROCODILES

. . . and while humans are not a traditional staple of a Nile crocodile's diet, there have been numerous accounts of them feasting on humans . . .

"See?" said Oliver.

"But this doesn't prove anything," said Archer. "It could still all be a lie."

"That's true," said Oliver. "But you heard what she said before. She's never attended a real school. She was tutored—probably because she was traveling the world."

"So why is she in a real school now?" asked Archer. "Why did she stop?"

"Her leg, of course. She stopped after the accident. That was enough to make her give it all up."

Archer wasn't sold.

"You at least have to admit that she was pretty incredible in class."

"I didn't notice anything special," said Archer.

"But Mrs. Murkley went after her and she didn't even blink. I would have collapsed into my shoes." Oliver placed a plaid cushion on his lap and traced the pattern with his finger. "You know," he continued. "She just might be the one who could—" He stopped and looked at Archer from the corner of his eye.

"Who could what?" asked Archer.

Oliver shrugged. "I forgot what I was saying. It's just—I don't think there's anyone in this school who has done the things she's done. And I *know* there was no one willing to do the thing she did."

"What did she do?"

"She took Mrs. Murkley off you. It was obvious. I don't know why she did that. But you can't deny that she did."

It was true. But if Archer was impressed, he hid it well as he lifted his feet and slumped deeper into the couch, dwelling on the mysterious crocodile girl. Oliver tucked the pillow behind his head and went back to dwelling on Mrs. Murkley. Between the two of them, the empty reading room brimmed with dwell.

✦ Size Small Blazer ✦

Adélaïde waited alone in the room after class. She knew with her leg, she wouldn't make it very far in the crowded halls. But once they fell silent, she ventured out, held up the note from Mrs. Thimbleton, and asked a janitor for directions to the library.

"I have no idea where that is," the janitor replied, looking terribly confused. "But if I had to guess, I would say it's somewhere in Thailand."

Now Adélaïde was confused. "*Thailand?*" she repeated, thinking this janitor was having a bit of fun with her. "The *library* is in Thailand?"

The janitor started laughing. "I'm sorry, my dear," he replied. "Between your accent and my old ears, I thought you asked about a *Thai ferry*. No, the library is much closer."

The janitor pointed his mop past her head. "Go down this corridor here and make a right at the end. You'll see a book request station on your left and you'll want to keep going through the next set of doors. On the other side, you'll come to a staircase. Go up three flights—*three*, mind you. At the top, there will be two more sets of doors. You'll want the doors on the right. Those will take you to the library."

Adélaïde blinked at him.

"It's a lot, isn't it?" The janitor splashed his mop into the bucket and said he'd walk with her.

"I've always suggested that they make a map of this place," he said, as they made their way down the corridor. "You should see the faces of the little ones when they first arrive. Horror. That's the only way to describe it."

"Are all schools this big?" Adélaïde asked.

"I'm not sure," he replied. "But before they fired me, I used to clean over at Rosewood Hospital. And as crazy as it sounds, this school makes that hospital look *tiny*. I have to say, the buildings feel oddly similar, though."

Adélaïde froze and tilted her head at the janitor. That's what she had been thinking earlier that morning. The Button Factory reminded her of the Paris hospital. She didn't like that.

"Is something wrong?" the janitor asked.

Adélaïde shook her head and they continued on.

"Why did they fire you?" she asked.

"Pigeons," he replied.

"Pigeons?"

"Yes, the creatures kept flying into the maternity ward, and I had a difficult time getting them out and cleaning up after them. They wanted someone younger and more up to the task." A mischievous smile stretched across his face. "Of course, I gave them a little piece of my mind before leaving. But now, I only clean here and at the museum."

When they reached the stairs, he repeated, "Three flights up and the doors on the right." Adélaïde thanked him and clomped up the stairs. She stepped into the library, passed the librarian's deserted desk, and wandered down rows of shelves. She poked her head into the reading room, glanced over at the empty couches and armchairs, and was about to leave when she spotted two heads only just visible over the back of a couch.

"What did she do?" said one of the heads.

"She took Mrs. Murkley off you," said the other. "It was obvious. I don't know why she did that. But you can't deny that she did."

Adélaïde couldn't see their faces, but was nearly certain the dark-haired one was the polar bear boy—the same boy she'd seen on the rooftop during her first night in Rosewood. She hesitated, not sure if she should introduce herself, but that's what she decided to do.

TOMP, TOMP, TOMP. "AH—HEM."

Archer and Oliver glanced up over the back of the couch. The crocodile girl was peering down at them. They straightened. Oliver rubbed his hair, which only made it worse. No one said a word for a moment or two, but it felt like five or six. Archer was trying to figure out how long she'd been standing there. Adélaïde was trying to figure out what to say. Oliver cleared his throat.

"Hello," he said, with a slight hesitation because this girl intimidated him a little. "I—*uh*—I like clouds, too."

"What's your name?" she asked.

"I'm Oliver Glub," he replied. Archer didn't say anything, so Oliver added, "And this is Archer Helmsley."

"I thought his name was Alfred," said Adélaïde.

Oliver grinned. "I don't know why Mrs. Murkley calls him that."

Archer wasn't amused. He remained silent. Adélaïde sat down in an armchair facing them.

"I thought there was going to be an explosion in class," Oliver continued. "At least until you stepped in. Well, after you stepped in I thought there would be another explosion. But Archer was lucky you did."

"She's worse than Mr. Stanislas," said Adélaïde.

Oliver didn't know who Mr. Stanislas was, but it had to be true.

"My name is Adélaïde Belmont, by the way," she said.

Archer listened to this exchange without adding a single word. He was too busy staring at Adélaïde's leg. *Crocodiles.*

He couldn't compete with that. When Adélaïde looked at him he smiled, but that was just a disguise. In that moment, Archer felt smaller than a thumbtack but just as pointed.

"I was fine," he said, pushing up from the couch. "I didn't need your help. I'm a Helmsley. And that means something. Besides, my head was almost eaten by a polar bear but I still have it." He pointed at her leg. "You didn't do so well with the crocodile, did you?"

Archer felt prickly after saying this and wished he hadn't. But he had and he didn't wait for a response before storming out of the reading room, looking more and more miserable with each step.

Oliver and Adélaïde exchanged glances.

"Sorry," said Oliver. "He's usually much nicer than that."

"Is he?"

"He is. But I'd better go, too." Oliver stood up and awkwardly stuck out his hand. Adélaïde shook it. "It was nice meeting you," he said, and took off after Archer.

Adélaïde sat quietly in the reading room, wondering if she had said something wrong. She wasn't alone. Miss Whitewood had watched the scene from behind a bookshelf and once Oliver was gone, she approached Adélaïde.

"Am I right to think you're the new girl?" she asked.

Adélaïde turned and looked at Miss Whitewood. Compared

with Mrs. Murkley, she thought Miss Whitewood's face shone like a million stars.

"Yes," she replied. "My name is Adélaïde."

"Well Adélaïde, I'm supposed to give you a tour, aren't I? Why don't we start in this room, which I'm sure you've already guessed is part of the library. I'm the librarian. My name is Miss Whitewood." Without asking, she took Adélaïde's hand. They left the reading room and wandered down the book aisles.

"I like your leg, by the way," said Miss Whitewood. "Is it oak?"

"I think so," Adélaïde replied.

• An Undesired Wobble •

Oliver sprinted down the sidewalk after Archer. Two blocks later, Archer was in sight, but Oliver's pace slowed and not because he was tired. Suddenly, Oliver stopped all together and threw himself behind a tree. He peered around the trunk, waiting for Archer to step into his house. And when he did, Oliver ducked into his. He needed time to think everything over.

Archer felt horrible as he climbed the foyer steps. The light was on beneath the door of his father's study and his mother was in the sitting room dusting a photo of his grandparents deep in the jungles of somewhere.

"There's a plate for you in the fridge," she said. "I have to go to Mrs. Leperton's tonight, and your father is working late. He has to appear in court tomorrow."

"I'm not feeling well," said Archer, nodding. "I'll be in my room."

He turned to continue up the stairs but his mother stopped him.

"Did you see Mrs. Murkley?" she asked.

Archer rubbed his arm and sighed. He'd seen Mrs. Murkley all right.

"And did you apologize?"

Archer bobbed his head up and down. "Yes," he replied.

"I'm sure she appreciated it. A new day for the two of you, yes?"

Archer didn't say anything.

"*Yes?*" she repeated.

"Yes, she thanked me," he lied, knowing his mother wouldn't want to hear anything else. He was right. Mrs. Helmsley smiled and said, "Very good." Archer trudged up the stairs, passing the polar bear on the way to his room.

"Good afternoon," said the bear.

Archer stopped, but he wasn't in the mood.

"You're not real," he said. "Nothing in Helmsley House is."

"It's true," the bear replied. "But we were all of us mighty fine creatures in our day. This one time in the Arctic I—"

"Why are you talking to me?" Archer asked.

"I'm not talking to you," said the bear. "You're using me to talk to yourself. Or perhaps you're using me to argue with yourself. Either way, I'm not saying anything. It's all you."

Archer opened his mouth and raised a finger but went no further.

"It is a little strange, isn't it?" said the bear.

"Am I crazy?" asked Archer.

That was really not the sort of question you should ever ask a stuffed polar bear. Still, Archer had nothing to worry about. Many people fear they might be crazy at some point in their lives, but it requires a healthy dose of sanity to think there's a chance you might be crazy. It's only when you think there is no chance whatsoever that you should be worried. Only you won't be worried because you'll be crazy.

"You're a little crazy," said the bear. "But if you ask me, that's for the best."

Archer lowered his finger and shut his mouth, thinking it better to say nothing more. He continued to his room, closed his door, and peeked across the gardens. Adélaïde's house was dark. He wished he hadn't said what he'd said, but jealousy makes the best of us sour with the milk.

Archer felt dizzy. He spread out on his bed. Everything was out of order. Nothing made sense. And he wanted something he understood. To one side of his bedroom was a bookshelf, built into the wall and stretching ten feet to the ceiling. Archer lifted his head. He had something on the top shelf—something he didn't want his mother to find. And though it was quite the process to retrieve it, Archer rolled off his bed and set to work. He dragged a small table to the foot of the bookshelf and began stacking chairs on top. Three did the job well enough. He then carefully climbed up the pile, stuck his hand over the dusty lip of the shelf, and removed a small turquoise box.

Archer opened the box. The glass eye looked up at him. His stomach tied itself in a knot. He missed his grandparents terribly. But before his thoughts could go any further, Archer froze. He felt a wobble. In and of themselves, wobbles are fine things. Wobbles happen all the time. But a wobble is most unwelcome when it originates from three chairs stacked atop a table with you at the pinnacle, eight feet up. There followed a second wobble. Archer closed his eyes. The glass eye couldn't. He clutched the box, and he and the tower collapsed to the floor.

• One-Legged French Girls •

Adélaïde followed Miss Whitewood out through the front doors of the Button Factory. They'd spoken about many things during their tour—about France and about being tutored at home—but not about bakery trucks or ballet. They stood on the front steps beneath the factory smokestacks.

"Well," said Miss Whitewood. "I do hope you'll enjoy it here."

"I think I will," Adélaïde lied.

"I also hope you'll come visit me during breaks if you can."

"I would like that," said Adélaïde.

They parted ways. Adélaïde walked north two blocks and down a narrow street called Howling Bloom, which was lined with many stores, including her father's new café—a corner shop painted an alluring yellow that seemed to glow as if by magic. She pressed her face to the glass. Mr. Belmont was working alone inside.

Opposite the café, two flights up, Molly S. Mellings spotted Adélaïde from a window of DuttonLick's sweetshop. She tossed a jelly bean at her and shouted, "It's the crocodile girl!"

Adélaïde spun around. The sweetshop windows swelled with Button Factory students—some stared in awe while others laughed and made loud chomping sounds. Adélaïde stepped over the jelly bean and into the café. She pulled herself atop a barstool and slid her hands beneath her thighs. Mr. Belmont filled a cup with boiling water.

"Black tea or green?" he asked.

"Black," she replied.

"Well?" he said, placing the cup in front of her and folding his arms. "How was it?"

Adélaïde shrugged and scooped a heap of sugar into the cup. "Fine, I suppose. But I don't want to go back there."

"Why not?" Mr. Belmont asked.

"I just don't like it, is all."

"You didn't like anything about it?"

Adélaïde lifted the cup to just below her lip. "Miss Whitewood was nice," she said, and after taking a sip, explained who Miss Whitewood was.

"Well," Mr. Belmont said, turning to continue polishing an espresso machine. "If you did leave school, what would you do?"

Adélaïde shrugged again. "Let's keep traveling. I'd rather not stay in one place for too long."

"We can't do that."

Adélaïde knew they couldn't. She spun the stool and glanced around the café. It was closed to the public, as her father was still setting everything up. Mr. Belmont was a very specific man and wanted everything just right, which meant he often did the work himself.

"Where's Pierre and Pierre?" she asked.

Mr. Belmont shook his head. "Home remodelers at my *dis*-service, you mean? I couldn't take it—all that finishing of each other's sentences. When they started finishing mine, I told them to leave."

Adélaïde was disappointed. She thought they were funny. Mr. Belmont bent down behind the counter and reemerged with a crate labeled "Espresso Cups."

"I met a man this morning," he said. "Lives just across the gardens. He has a son about your age—also attends the Willow Academy."

Adélaïde spun back around. "*Archer Helmsley,*" she said.

"So you've met him?"

She nodded. "He's rude and I think he owns a polar bear."

Mr. Belmont laughed. "I did catch a glimpse of their house. It's called Helmsley House. Peculiar place. Lots of animals. I didn't realize who they were at first, but then I remembered reading about the grandparents. They were explorers—floated out to sea atop an iceberg."

Adélaïde lowered her cup. Until this, she hadn't been sure what Mrs. Murkley had been talking about. Now it made sense. Or at least as much sense as floating out to sea atop an iceberg could.

"Are they dead?" she asked.

"That's the assumption. Don't think anyone has seen them since it happened."

Adélaïde finished her tea in silence.

"And perhaps he's just shy," said Mr. Belmont after a moment. "This Archer Helmsley. After all, not all of us can be bold French girls."

"Or one-legged French girls," Adélaïde mumbled.

She thanked her father and slid off the stool.

"I'll be home soon," Mr. Belmont said.

Adélaïde nodded and left the café. She slipped quickly beneath DuttonLick's and clomped her way back to North Willow Street, thinking about this possibly not-so-rude Archer Helmsley whose grandparents had floated out to sea atop an iceberg. Adélaïde didn't think such things could happen. But two years ago, she also didn't think pigeons could send a bakery truck crashing into a lamppost.

✦ Petrified Glub ✦

Oliver finished his dinner and opened the garden door. Mr. Glub picked up his newspaper and looked at his watch.

"Shouldn't you be going to the roof?" he asked.

"Not tonight," said Oliver. He shut the door behind him and went to the corner of the garden. On the ground, embedded in the grass, was a moss-covered stone with the name *Théo* etched into it.

Théo was Oliver's cat—his first pet. And Théo had been a good cat, most helpful with keeping the basement mice from overtaking the house (a war the Glubs had been losing of late). But when Oliver was seven, instead of eating a basement mouse, Théo scratched open a bag of cement mix and for reasons Oliver still couldn't figure out, Théo found the mixture to his taste. Oliver found Théo an hour later and called to him, but the cat didn't move. He tried to pick him up but he couldn't. Théo was petrified. Oliver sighed and lay down in the grass.

Rising above his garden wall loomed the Murkley house, with lights beaming like interrogation lamps. Mrs. Murkley petrified him. He was glad he wasn't on her list, but Archer was, and for the first time, he realized that simply being Archer's sidekick could get him into very real and serious trouble. He wasn't cut out for this line of work. Adélaïde was. He'd only accepted Archer's request because he wanted a friend. Adélaïde could actually help Archer. And if she did, Oliver wanted no part of it.

A firefly dotted past and made Oliver smile. He went back inside, found an empty mason jar in the pantry, poked holes in the top with a pen, and was about to return to the garden when he decided to make a quick trip to the roof to see Archer. He climbed the ladder and peered over the edge, but Archer wasn't there.

CHAPTER

ELEVEN

• Insult to Injury •

Archer opened his eyes. He was lying on the floor in the aftermath of the wobble. He decided to stay there awhile and stared at the ceiling. He knew it was a ceiling. He'd been staring at this one for eleven years. And now more than ever, Archer wanted to smash through it and soar far beyond the clouds, far beyond the stars, and straight into the vast who knows what. But he couldn't do that so he stayed where he was, staring up into that great white nothingness. All at once, a head sprouted from nowhere.

"Your ceiling is pretty nice," said Oliver. "But I think mine is better."

Archer smiled and took Oliver's hand. But he was still spinning from the crash and only able to rise halfway.

"Are you okay?" Oliver asked, looking around at the mess.

"I'm fine," said Archer, rubbing a bump on the back of his head.

"But what happened?"

Archer was about to explain, but before he could, a paper airplane floated in through the window and jabbed him in the back of the head. Oliver picked it up.

"What's that?" Archer asked.

"A brochure," said Oliver, unfolding the paper "For something called *Belmont Coffee*." He turned to Archer. "What's Belmont Coffee?"

Archer didn't know. He stumbled to his feet to see where this plane had come from, but he was struck once more. This time it was a direct hit to his forehead.

"Does this happen every night?" asked Oliver.

Archer bent down to pick up the second plane. This one wasn't a brochure. This was a *bonjour*.

"There's your answer," said Oliver, looking out from the balcony door and across the gardens where the crocodile girl was standing on her balcony. She smiled and waved. Archer and Oliver waved back.

"Now she's taunting me with paper airplanes," said Archer.

Oliver disagreed. "*Bonjour* means hello," he said. "If she meant that to be a taunt, it's not a very good one."

"No, she's taunting me."

"I'm surprised she's even talking to you," said Oliver, finally putting his hand down. "You were rude before and there was no reason for it."

Archer left the doorway to search for his glass eye in the rubble.

"I should have said it earlier," Oliver continued. "And I'm surprised you don't see it, but I think she's the one you're looking for—the one who can help you."

Archer picked up his glass eye and said, "I don't need her help."

"Of course you do," Oliver replied, still staring at Adélaïde. "At least, if you're as serious about Antarctica as you were before. That girl has sailed across Egypt in a hot air balloon and survived Nile crocodiles. *And* she willingly took on Mrs. Murkley. Those are just the parts we know. Me? Well, I'm good at falling down stairs." Oliver wrinkled his brow at Archer. "Why don't you want her help?"

"Because I don't think it's true," said Archer.

"You're not acting like that," said Oliver. "You seem jealous." He glanced once more at Adélaïde. "But maybe it isn't true. You should ask her if you want to know for sure."

Archer sat down on his bed, uncertain what he believed.

But Oliver was right. He'd been jealous of Adélaïde. He rubbed his arm and nodded at Oliver's hand.

"Why are you holding that jar?" he asked.

Oliver had forgotten about his jar. "I was in the middle of something," he said. "I can't stay. I just wanted to tell you what I told you and don't worry if you'd prefer her help and not mine. We both know you'll need someone with experience." He paused, then added, "But I still don't think you should do it."

Oliver returned to his garden, and Archer slipped off his bed and went to the balcony door. Adélaïde was leaning against her balcony railing watching Oliver. There was no getting around it; this girl looked nothing like a great adventurer. She was small and skinny and perhaps a little dainty, if dainty is the right word. Dainty people don't become explorers. And if they do, they don't make it very far. But perhaps Oliver was right about that, too. Perhaps the unlikeliness of it meant it was true. These sorts of things do happen. You'll see someone odd and tell your friends, "She eats lizards." But then you'll discover *she* happens to be the greatest pastry chef in the city and you'll be the one left alone to eat your lizards.

Archer rolled the glass eye from one hand to the other. It watched him as he did so and he knew what it was thinking.

You don't look like a great adventurer either. That was true. And if he was going to be one, he would need help. Maybe Adélaïde *was* the one to do that. He needed to know if the crocodile rumor was true, or if Adélaïde was just some scantily dressed emperor wandering the Button Factory halls.

Archer tore a page from his notebook and wrote Adélaïde a note. He folded it into a plane and sent it sailing across the gardens. It was a good throw. Adélaïde jumped to catch it and stood quietly for a moment after reading it.

Did a crocodile really eat your leg?

Adélaïde disappeared inside her bedroom where she sat a few moments more before returning to the balcony and sending another plane to Archer.

Yes

Archer bit his lip. It was all there in black and white. Three letters. One syllable. He looked from Adélaïde to the airplane and then to the glass eye. It *did* make sense. He sent another plane flying and left his room without awaiting a reply.

• Glass Eyes Hear No Lies •

Archer hurried down the stairs in perfect silence. The light was still on beneath the door to his father's study, and his mother was next door at Mrs. Leperton's. He creaked down the cellar stairs and reappeared with a ladder.

"It's escaping!" shouted the ostrich. "Quick! Someone grab it! The thing with dirty hands is escaping!"

Archer maneuvered the ladder through the conservatory, past the *shudderflies*, and out into the garden. There was no way for him to know if his grandparents were still alive. Some days he thought so and other days he didn't. But ever since that night on the rooftop, the night when Oliver had suggested they dig into the ice, Archer thought that their being alive was a real possibility. And if they were alive, and if they returned to Helmsley House, everything would change.

They had to return. Even if that meant he had to bring them home himself.

Archer leaned the ladder against the wall at the back of the garden and climbed to the top. On the other side, Adélaïde was standing in the grass staring up at him. He waved awkwardly and said, "Hello."

"Hello again," she replied.

For a moment, that was that. Archer stood atop the ladder

staring down at Adélaïde, who stood in the grass looking up at him.

"I want to apologize for before," Archer continued. "For what I said about the polar bear and the crocodile and your leg and everything."

Adélaïde nodded. "It's fine," she replied.

"My polar bear isn't real anyway," said Archer. "None of the animals in my house are. They couldn't chew my head off even if they wanted to."

Adélaïde smiled.

"But your crocodile was real and I think you did better than I would have in that situation."

"I froze," she said.

"I think most people would their first time. The second time will be different."

"I don't think there will be a second time," she replied.

Archer was afraid of this—afraid that Adélaïde would not want to go on another adventure. But he had an idea. He fumbled in his pocket and removed a box.

"Heads up," he said, and dropped it down to her.

"What's this?" she asked.

"Open it."

Adélaïde opened the box and what she thought was a large marble rolled out onto her palm.

"It's pretty," she said.

"It's a glass eye," he replied.

Adélaïde quickly rolled it back into the box and discreetly wiped her hand against her dress.

"Thank you," she said, though it sounded more like a question.

"It's from my grandparents. They were great explorers so I thought you might like it."

"Which of them lost an eye?"

"Neither," said Archer. "It belonged to a ship's captain. He only had one eye. I think I met him, but that might have been a coincidence."

Adélaïde looked horrified.

Archer was confused. "Are you okay?" he asked.

"Why did they take his eye?!"

Archer shook his head and grinned. "No, they didn't *take* it from him. He *gave* it to them so they would remember seeing a mountain."

Archer explained that the captain only had one eye but still captained his ship. And while the gift wasn't terribly subtle, Adélaïde appreciated it.

"Thank you," she said.

After that, Archer chose his words carefully, thinking it best to begin vague and then slowly work into the specifics.

"I gave you that because there's somewhere I want to go, but it's far away and I was hoping you would help me because—"

"Okay," said Adélaïde.

Archer raised an eyebrow. "What's that?" he asked.

"I said 'okay.'"

"Okay what?"

"Okay, I'll help you."

Archer didn't understand. "But you don't even know what I need help with," he said.

"You want to go somewhere far away," she replied.

"But I didn't say where."

"That doesn't matter."

Was it really that easy or was the crocodile girl making fun of him? He couldn't tell.

"Are you laughing at me?" he asked.

"I'm not," she replied.

"But a crocodile ate your leg."

"That was two years ago."

"And you're still interested?"

"Very much."

It all made perfect sense to Adélaïde. Adélaïde knew where she didn't want to go. She didn't want to go back to the Button Factory. It reminded her of the hospital. And beyond that, she was once a ballerina and sitting perfectly still at a desk all day was simply no good. The truth was Archer could have said he was going to the moon and Adélaïde would have wanted to come along.

"But just out of curiosity," she said. "Where is it that you want to go?"

Just then Oliver poked his head over the garden wall. Oliver had climbed his tree with one hand because in his other was a jar aglow with fireflies. He looked annoyed.

"I don't mean to be rude," he said. "But would you mind keeping it down?" He nodded toward the Murkley residence. "I really don't want her coming out here and taking another swing at me with that shovel."

Archer pulled himself atop the garden wall to get a better look at Oliver's jar. The neon critters were blinking and bouncing all around. Archer was very little the last time he had hunted a firefly.

"Have you ever hunted a firefly?" he asked Adélaïde.

She hadn't.

"Can we join you?" Archer asked.

Oliver shrugged. "I think I have more jars," he said.

• A Trio •

It took a concerted effort getting Adélaïde and her wooden leg quietly over the garden wall, but with an extra ladder from Oliver, they managed just fine.

"Your garden looks like a jungle," she said, taking Oliver's hand.

"We try our best," he replied. "There's just no controlling it."

Archer stood atop the wall, lifting the ladder up out of his garden. He lowered it to Adélaïde and then started down Oliver's ladder, but paused when he heard a door open. Two gardens over, Mrs. Leperton and Mrs. Helmsley stepped outside. Archer stood frozen in plain sight, watching his mother with eyes wide. And though she didn't notice him, he made a terrible decision. He jumped back, causing the ladder to pull away from the wall. Oliver and Adélaïde quickly took hold of the bottom, and for a moment the ladder and Archer stood straight up in the air. But the teetering weight was too much. They couldn't hold on. Archer took one last look at them before crashing to the ground.

"What was that!" Mrs. Leperton cried.

"I have no idea!" said Mrs. Helmsley.

Oliver and Adélaïde were silent, staring at a motionless Archer lying beneath the ladder.

"I think it came from the Glubs'," Mrs. Helmsley said.

"It's their own fault," agreed Mrs. Leperton. "Can't expect to see where you're going in a garden like that."

✦

Archer groaned as Adélaïde and Oliver pulled the ladder off his face. He was having a rough day. This fall hurt more than the bookshelf catastrophe, and the bump on his head doubled in size. He opened his eyes. Adélaïde was kneeling over him.

"Hello," he groaned.

"You have grass in your teeth," she replied, pointing to hers. "Here and here."

Archer rubbed his mouth. "Did I get it?" he asked.

Adélaïde nodded. "But there's also a long wooden sliver sticking out of your cheek. Hold still." Adélaïde gently removed the wooden splinter and wiped his cheek. "There's a bit of blood," she said. "Did you fall on purpose?"

"It was my mother," he replied, rubbing the cut. "She can't see me out here with the lad—" His eyes opened wide. "Are they still over there?"

"No," said Oliver. "They're gone."

"Why can't she see you with a ladder?" Adélaïde asked.

"It's a long story," said Archer.

Adélaïde helped him to his feet. Archer shook his head a few times as they tucked the ladders against the garden wall. Oliver went inside to find two more jars and quickly returned, handing them one each.

The evening air was heavy over the Willow Street gardens and made them feel like they were standing inside a bubble.

Droplets beaded on the grass and glazed Adélaïde's shoes as she crept toward the back corner of the garden, following the dotted path of a firefly. She stood perfectly still; then, as quickly as she could, capped the jar and trapped a neon critter inside.

"Got one!" she cried.

"Shhh!" shushed Oliver, pointing once more to the Murkley house.

Archer did the same, pointing to his house.

Adélaïde made a face at them and looked at her firefly. Below the jar, next to her foot, she spotted a moss-covered stone.

"Who's Théo?" she asked.

Oliver sighed at the question.

"He doesn't want to talk about it," said Archer, who still knew nothing about Théo either. He showed his jar to Adélaïde. It was brimming with fireflies. "And you can make your fingers glow if you pinch them," he said.

"Thanks for the tip," she replied. "But I think I'm okay."

As the three scurried this way and that across the garden, Oliver's younger sister Claire watched with her face pressed to the second-floor window. "Hello, Archer!" was her muffled cry through the glass. Archer waved. The non-nocturnal opossum sauntered along the garden walls without anyone's notice, searching for a place to settle in before nightfall.

After collecting their fill, Archer, Oliver, and Adélaïde sat down in the grass next to the shaggy tree.

"What was it like being in a hot air balloon over Egypt?" Archer asked.

"The stars were quite pretty," said Adélaïde.

"That's what my grandparents said."

"Where else have you been?" Oliver asked.

Adélaïde was silent. Archer looked at her. She seemed to be having a difficult time remembering all the places she'd been, but once she started naming them, she quickly remembered more and more, and Archer and Oliver were impressed.

"Your father took you?" Archer asked.

"No, he's in the coffee business," said Adélaïde. "My mother took me." She paused, then added, "They used to call her the snail because she took her house wherever she went—always packed and ready to go."

"Was she with you when the crocodile ate your leg?"

Adélaïde nodded. "She fell too while trying to grab me."

"Did it hurt?" Oliver asked.

"It happened quickly. It's all a blur. I don't remember it well."

"I hope I never get that close to a crocodile," said Oliver.

THÉO

"They're dangerous. It swallowed my mother in two bites."

Archer and Oliver lowered their jars. "Is that true?" both asked.

"Don't worry," she replied. "I didn't like her anyway."

"You didn't like her even though she tried to stop you falling out of the balloon?" Oliver asked.

Adélaïde bit her lip. "It's complicated," she said, and quickly changed the subject. "Did your grandparents really float out to sea atop an iceberg?"

Archer nodded and explained the story.

"That's why they keep me inside," he said. "They think I'd do something equally dangerous if I had the chance."

Oliver pinched his lips. "They're right about that," he said.

"It doesn't matter," Archer replied. "Everything is going to be different when my grandparents return."

"You think they're still alive?" Adélaïde asked.

Tonight, Archer was certain of it.

A cry shot from the Murkley household and pierced the bubble over their heads.

"She reminds me of the Mouse King," said Adélaïde.

Oliver shook his head. "She's the Queen of Hearts," he said. "She nearly chopped my head off."

"She's worse than the Queen of Hearts," said Archer. "She

doesn't just want to chop off our heads. She wants to put hers in their place."

Adélaïde started giggling and she couldn't stop.

"What's so funny?" Archer asked.

"I was picturing Mrs. Murkley's head on your body," she giggled.

Oliver giggled, too. Archer turned it into a trio.

"It wouldn't be very pretty, would it?" he said, lifting his firefly jar to his eyes and tapping at the glass.

"Are you kidding?" said Adélaïde, trying to stop a second bout of laughter from erupting. "It would be terrifying!"

"I'd never sleep again," agreed Oliver.

Archer's eyes began sparkling and his fingers began twitching, and he was speaking very softly to himself but he was not a million miles away.

"She's not going to have the chance," he said.

"*Oh*, I think she'll try," said Oliver.

"She certainly will," agreed Adélaïde.

"But we'll be long gone," said Archer.

Four eyebrows went up.

"Where will we be?" Adélaïde asked.

Archer looked at her and smiled.

✦ Part Three ✦

THE JOURNEY BEGINS

CHAPTER

TWELVE

• The Journey Begins •

Preparing an expedition is no small undertaking. Expeditions require thoughtful work and organization. This much Archer knew and he wasted little time putting a plan in order.

"I know I said I've been lots of places," said Adélaïde. "But I don't think I can help you with this."

"Don't worry," said Archer. "What's important is that you've done other things because I've done nothing."

Member of the Rosewood Public Library

Willow Academy Library

• BOOK REQUEST CARD •

Request No. 37955

Miss Whitewood,

Can you please find every book you have on Antarctica?

Thank you,

Archer Helmsley

"Should I be worried?" asked Miss Whitewood. She placed her hand on Adélaïde's shoulder. "I hope they're not dragging you into anything."

Oliver frowned. "No offense, Miss Whitewood, but I don't think that's possible."

Miss Whitewood pointed to a table holding a massive stack of books. "That's everything I could find," she said.

Archer reviewed the stack. It would require prioritizing. He divvied up the books and they carried them into the reading room. The janitor was dusting a windowsill as they entered. He chuckled when he saw Adélaïde.

"How was that Thai Ferry?" he asked.

Adélaïde smiled. "Very nice."

"She's been to Thailand, too?" whispered Oliver.

"I guess so," said Archer.

In the weeks that followed, the trio spent much of their time in the reading room and students' room before, between, and after class, reading as many books on Antarctica as they could.

Many of the books were old and dense and tedious, to say the least. Archer was fine with this. Oliver and Adélaïde grew bored. They sorted through the stacks, placing the boring books next to Archer and the books with photos and diagrams next to themselves. Archer made notes in his journal as he read. He shared the important notes with the others, but thought it best to keep the more terrible details to himself.

1914. Antarctic. 69° 5 S, 51° 30 W
The ship Endurance *was trapped in ice. The ice squeezed the ship.*
Sounded like, "Heavy fireworks and blasting of guns."
The ship sank. The crew were stranded.

"Hopefully, the worst part will be the Drake Passage," he said. "But once we're past that, the rest should be fine."

"I don't get it," said Oliver.

Archer glanced over his notes. "It says the Drake Passage is—"

"No, I got that," said Oliver. "What I don't get is why seals start out all fluffy and white and then turn into giant sausages."

"Sausages with teeth," said Adélaïde.

"Focus," said Archer, catching a glimpse of Oliver's book. He tilted his head. "It really does look like a sausage."

"They're up to something strange," said Alice P. Suggins. "We should tell Mrs. Murkley. She might reward us."

"I'm not saying anything to her," said Charlie H. Brimble. "She makes my thoughts get all confused."

"It's true," said Molly S. Mellings. "We'd accidentally say that we were the ones up to something strange."

Charlie leaned against the back of the couch and skimmed a page over Adélaide's shoulder.

"Antarctica?" he said. "Are you hoping to lose your other leg?"

Oliver lowered his book and glared at Charlie. "Why don't you go play with your chickens, *String Bean*?" he said.

Archer started laughing. Adélaïde giggled, too. Charlie slunk away. Adélaïde suggested they sneak out of the Button Factory during lunch and go to her father's café, where they could speak without anyone overhearing.

"What about your father overhearing?" asked Archer.

"He only underhears," said Adélaïde.

• Subtle Hints of Orange Peel •

Archer said their best escape option would be an exit near the northwest corner of the courtyard. This wing of the Button Factory was mostly storage rooms, which meant fewer teachers to catch them, and a tunnel led from the courtyard, through the building, and out onto the street. So as the students made their way to the dining hall, the trio broke ranks, scurried across the courtyard, around the crumbling fountain, and through the tunnel. From there, it was only two blocks north to Howling Bloom Street and Mr. Belmont's café.

"It is a pleasure to meet you, Archer," said Mr. Belmont. He turned to Oliver. "And you are?"

Oliver shrugged. "I'm just a Glub," he replied.

"Oliver Glub," said Adélaïde.

"*Glub?*" repeated Mr. Belmont. "That's an intriguing name. Yes, well, very good."

The café was crowded, but the patrons were too busy drinking coffee and reading newspapers to pay them any mind. Archer noticed the flowery woman sitting in the corner drinking enough espresso to kill a small hippopotamus. But after their third lunchtime visit, even he developed a taste for that potent brew. Mr. Belmont was pleased.

"You might like this one, too," he said, placing another cup in front of Archer. "That will get the mind soaring high above the clouds on subtle hints of orange peel."

During their lunches, they continued to discuss the matter at hand. One day Archer brought maps of Antarctica that he found in the map room of Helmsley House. They pushed aside their cups and plates and spread the maps over the table.

"That's Antarctica?" said Oliver. "It's gigantic."

"It is rather large," agreed Adélaïde.

"It'll be fine," said Archer. "Ships at sea must follow specific routes like cars on roads, so any ship we take should follow the same path my grandparents did."

"But icebergs float," said Oliver. "It won't be in the same place."

"Maybe it will have come full circle," said Adélaïde. "And be where it was two years ago."

Archer lowered his third espresso with a shaky hand. "I don't know," he said. "If it's there it's there and if it's not it's not, but there's really no sense—no sense at all in wondering what will be until we're there. I think it's there. It has to be there. You know?"

Adélaïde pulled the cup away from him. "I think you've had enough of that," she said.

• Caramel Cream & Ice Schemes •

On their way back to the Button Factory, the trio sometimes stopped across the street at DuttonLick's for something sweet. Oliver was right. It was a terrific shop with windows displaying all sorts of delights, and the thick aroma of chocolate to greet their noses as they stepped inside. Spiraling up to the ceiling were racks of lollipops, dollops of taffy, and great mountains of chocolate bars.

Oliver preferred to take his time, but Archer knew being late to Mrs. Murkley's class would be a mistake.

"How about candied cherries?" he asked, trying to hurry Oliver along.

Oliver was incredulous. "Candied cherries!" he repeated. "No one enters DuttonLick's to buy something as boring as candied cherries!"

"Well, what do you want?" said Adélaïde, inspecting a row of sea-green seahorse lollipops.

Oliver wanted the whole store, but settled for a caramel cream chocolate bar. They paid for the chocolate and headed back to the Button Factory. Oliver broke the bar into three parts and they walked in silence as the chocolate and caramel cream melted in their mouths. They passed beneath the archway and stepped into the courtyard, joining the other students heading to afternoon class.

"Does your father have a freezer at his shop?" Archer asked.

"I don't think so," said Adélaïde. "Why?"

"Because we have no experience with Antarctic temperatures. Not even close. And I think we should at least have some sense of what that will be like."

"We could do something with ice after school," Adélaïde suggested.

It wasn't a terrible idea but they couldn't do it that day.

"Archer and I have something *personal* we have to do today," said Oliver, trying his best to look casual about it.

"Something important," Archer added.

Adélaïde shrugged. "That's fine," she said. "We'll do it tomorrow."

They made it to class just as Mrs. Murkley returned from the teachers' lounge.

• An Unsavory Alliance •

Mrs. Murkley had not softened since that first day of school. The students tried their best to resist a cough or a sneeze, fearing even these would land them in a heap of trouble. They were right. Digby Fig spent an entire afternoon scraping gum off the bottom of Mrs. Murkley's desk when he was unable to stop hiccupping. The students suppressed their grins as each hiccup caused Digby to smack his head against the underside of the desk.

During Mrs. Murkley's classes, Oliver distanced himself from Archer and Adélaïde. He was afraid Mrs. Murkley would make a connection between them. But Mrs. Murkley was no fool. She suspected an unsavory alliance was forming after spotting the trio numerous times in the corridors and library. Archer was unaware of this until he spotted her in the library that afternoon.

"Still just the librarian, I see," Mrs. Murkley said as she approached Miss Whitewood's desk.

Miss Whitewood smiled politely. "Can I help you find a book?" she asked. "Do you have something specific in mind?"

"Of course I do," huffed Mrs. Murkley. "It's dangerous business leaving your mind open around books. I require a text on the colonial uprisings—the role the French played and how the British dealt with them."

Archer slipped out from behind the bookshelf and into the reading room.

"I'll see what I can find," Miss Whitewood said.

As Miss Whitewood scoured the shelves, Mrs. Murkley strolled toward the reading room.

"Close your books!" whispered Archer.

"Why?" asked Oliver.

There was not time to explain. He grabbed Oliver's book and tossed it behind the couch. Adélaïde quickly shut hers. Archer slid his notebook into his pocket and sat down. When Mrs. Murkley stepped into the room, Oliver took his strategy to a new level and nearly fell off the couch.

"Just as I suspected!" Mrs. Murkley announced proudly, towering over them. "And *what*, may I ask, are you three up to?"

"*Two*," clarified Oliver. "I'm not with them."

Adélaïde jabbed him and beamed at Mrs. Murkley. "We're keeping our heads where our heads ought to be," she said.

"In books," added Archer. "Books that have nothing to do with polar bears."

"Or guillotines," said Adélaïde.

"Or icebergs," mumbled Oliver.

Mrs. Murkley leaned forward to grab Adélaïde's book, but Adélaïde pulled it tight to her stomach.

"I've found a few books for you, Margery!" Miss Whitewood called from her desk.

Mrs. Murkley gave all three a contemptuous eye before leaving. Adélaïde gave that same eye to Oliver.

"*Two?*" she repeated. "You stand up to the String Bean but not her?"

"She has a lot more hip and shoulder," said Oliver.

"Don't worry," said Archer. "But we have to be more careful."

"And we'd better go," said Oliver. "Archer and I have that *personal* thing we need to do."

• An Ice Gift •

The following day after school, Adélaïde and Oliver climbed down the ladder to Archer's bedroom. Archer had three coolers lined up. Adélaïde unzipped her bag and handed out earmuffs, gloves, and scarves. Archer opened the coolers and they all sat down.

"What exactly are we doing?" Oliver asked.

"I guess we'll just eat as much as we can," said Archer.

As they began to do just that, there was a knock at the door. Oliver and Adélaïde dashed behind the bed. Mr. Helmsley entered to ask Archer why there was a trail of water leading from the kitchen to his bedroom.

"What are you doing?" Mr. Helmsley asked slowly when he saw Archer in earmuffs, sitting before a cooler of ice.

Archer knew there was nothing he could say that would make this look any less unusual, so he told the truth.

"Eating ice," he replied.

". . . Eating ice?" repeated Mr. Helmsley. He shook his head. *And she thinks it's for the best we keep him locked in here*. "Well, I'm glad to see you're keeping busy."

Archer, Oliver, and Adélaïde continued eating ice after Mr. Helmsley left, but ten minutes later, they'd all had enough.

"This was a terrible idea," said Adélaïde.

Oliver was oscillating between this world and the next. Adélaïde smacked his back and an ice cube shot out of his mouth.

"Thanks," he sputtered.

"I guess we can try it again some other time," said Archer, pulling off his earmuffs. "Unless we find a better way."

Oliver stood up. "I'm going to get some tea to bring us back to room temperature," he said.

Archer and Adélaïde waited on the roof while Oliver went to his kitchen, but for cake, not for tea. Today was Adélaïde's eleventh birthday, though she made no mention of it. Mr. Belmont, however, had discreetly told Archer the date during one of their café meetings. So Archer and Oliver had spent the previous afternoon doing something *personal*. They'd spent the afternoon with Mrs. Glub in the Glubs' kitchen learning how to make a cake.

"Now it's not very complicated," said Mrs. Glub. "But timing is everything. Archer, you get three eggs and Oliver, two cups of flour."

Making a cake might not be a complicated process, but there will always be a few kinks the first time you try anything. Mr. Glub spotted a few kinks the moment he stepped into the kitchen.

"That's, uh—we're not going to eat that, are we?" he asked.

"Does it look that bad?" said Archer.

"Well," said Mrs. Glub. "I can't say it's what I was picturing, but there's a lot of heart in that cake."

Oliver agreed. "I think it looks good," he said.

Oliver returned to the rooftop with the large Glub and Helmsley original cake. Adélaïde stared at them both.

"Your father told us," said Archer. "Sorry I made you eat ice on your birthday."

Oliver set the cake on the chimney. "Don't worry," he said. "This will taste better."

If you tipped your head to the left and closed one eye, it looked just like a store-bought cake. And it did taste better than ice, which Oliver was glad to hear.

"The peanut butter and blueberry filling is wonderfully original," said Adélaïde.

"We tried to follow the recipe," said Archer. "But lost it halfway through."

"I'm not good at following plans anyway," said Oliver.

"What did you wish for?" Archer asked.

"A *bon voyage*," said Adélaïde.

"Thanks for that," said Oliver.

"Thanks for this," said Adélaïde, taking another bite.

CHAPTER THIRTEEN

• A Not-So-Good Plan •

The weeks passed from one to the next and it was nearing the end of September. Archer had spent a considerable amount of time trying to work out the specifics of how they would actually pull this journey off. There were two issues. They needed both a departure date for a ship going to Antarctica, and equipment. He knew the ship would have almost everything they needed, but thought it best to have a few things of their own just in case something went wrong as it had for his grandparents. The problem was that this would require a trip into Rosewood—a trip that would be more difficult than sneaking out of the Button Factory or into Oliver's house. But Archer had an idea. He asked Oliver and Adélaïde to meet him on the rooftop early one Saturday morning.

Oliver struggled up the ladder with a bowl of oranges

and three plates. Adélaïde spread a cloth over the table and opened a brown paper bag.

"What are those?" Oliver asked.

"Chocolate croissants. You'll like them."

The two had been bringing provisions to the roof for quite some time.

"Is that everything?" Adélaïde asked.

It was everything: chocolate croissants, tea and oranges, toast with butter and toast with jam, three soft-boiled eggs, undercooked bacon, some leftover birthday cake, and a little espresso. Oliver and Adélaïde were both quite proud of this spread until Archer jumped over the crack between the houses with a cooler and a disapproving frown.

"Is something wrong?" Adélaïde asked.

Archer lowered the cooler. "Why's all this food here?" he asked.

"You said you wanted to have a nice breakfast while you explained the next step."

Archer shook his head. There had been a misunderstanding. He thought they should try eating an *ice* breakfast, but there was a noticeable drop in morale after he said this. Oliver looked especially disappointed. He'd just spent the hour under Adélaïde's instruction trudging up and down four flights of stairs with all the food.

"*Ice* breakfast?" Oliver repeated, glancing over the delicious table.

Archer nodded, but he was now thinking the same thing Oliver was. "This does look much better," Archer admitted, pushing the cooler under the table. "We can eat the ice later."

Oliver and Adélaïde were relieved. They all sat down to feast, and for a while did so in silence. It was still early morning and most of the city was asleep. But the sun was beginning to rise and the trio was glowing a brilliant orange.

Adélaïde poured her tea into a bowl and drank. Oliver lowered his croissant.

"You're doing it wrong," he said. "Why are you drinking from a bowl?"

"This is how we do it in France," she replied.

Oliver grinned and held out a spoon. "Would you like this as well?"

Adélaïde bounced an orange peel off his forehead and into his cup. Oliver used the spoon to fish it out. Archer finished his croissant and brushed the flakes from his fingers.

"Adélaïde is the only one who's ever been to Rosewood Port," he said. "Do you think you can get us inside?"

Adélaïde stirred her tea and nodded. "We're small

enough," she said. "I doubt the guards would even notice."

Oliver's cheeks bulged with croissant. "But if you do get inside," he said, "then what are you going to do?"

"We'll have to find a ship to stow away on," said Archer.

Somehow he would have to figure out if and when a ship was leaving for Antarctica, and they could board that ship while the cargo was being loaded. Rosewood Port was large and heavily trafficked with ships docking and departing every day.

"There must be at least one heading to Antarctica in the near future," said Archer.

"But if not," said Adélaïde, "we can always take any ship as long as it goes south. Then change at another port to another ship that would go even farther south to Antarctica."

Archer agreed and took out his notebook. He flipped through the pages.

"But how are you going to know when a ship is leaving?" Oliver asked.

Adélaïde studied him. "Why do you keep saying *you*?" she asked. "Don't you mean *we*?"

Archer wasn't paying attention. His first concern was finding equipment. The night before, he'd rummaged through the map room looking for anything that might help him. Mostly he'd found dust, but he'd also stumbled onto a box with cards inside it. Each card listed the name, address, and account number of various shops around Rosewood. Some were very strange, but Archer found one that he thought was important. He slipped that card out of his notebook and handed it to Adélaïde.

"I found that last night," he said. "I'm sure you've been to stores like this before. I haven't, but I think we can find what we need in there, right?"

Strait *of* Magellan

EXPEDITION EQUIPMENT

– 17 Barrow's Strip –

Name(s): Ralph / Rachel Helmsley
Account Number: 39504728

"This should be good," said Adélaïde, still wondering what she had gotten herself into. "You want to go and have a look?"

"Yes," said Archer. "And we can ask them about docking schedules at Rosewood Port. I'll bet they'll know something."

This was the first step of Archer's plan. Overall, it wasn't a very good plan. But it's better to have a not very good plan than no plan at all.

Oliver disagreed.

✦ Cream of Tomato Soup ✦

Oliver had made a decision the night of the firefly hunt, but still had said nothing to Archer. His window of opportunity was quickly closing, so he decided that now was the time. He pulled a newspaper clipping from his pocket, flattened it against his leg, and handed it to Archer.

"I've liked spending time with you both," he said. "But I have to stop at the water's edge. I'm not going to Antarctica. That will explain why."

THE DOLDRUMS PRESS

CREAM OF TOMATO SOUP

. . . Family stunned when "Lionhearted" Uncle Baxley was found face-first in his cream of tomato soup at the age of forty-three . . .

Archer wasn't surprised. With a healthy diet and ample exercise, a lion's heart can last up to fifteen years. Mr. Baxley's made it to forty-three.

"That's not the point," said Oliver.

"What's the point?" Adélaïde asked.

"The point," said Oliver, "is that some people's hearts can handle more than others'. A year with Mrs. Murkley is plenty for me. I can't handle much more and I don't want to die in a bowl of cream of tomato soup."

"But you don't eat cream of tomato soup," said Archer.

"I don't like it much either," said Adélaïde.

"The kind of soup doesn't matter," said Oliver. "I don't want to die in any kind of soup or on an iceberg in Antarctica. I can't handle that. And to be honest, you shouldn't be doing this either." He turned to Adélaïde. "Did he tell you what will happen when his plan fails?"

"*If* the plan fails," said Archer.

"What will happen?" Adélaïde asked.

Archer was silent.

"His mother will ship him off to Raven Wood!" said Oliver.

"Raven Wood?" she repeated.

"Yes," said Oliver. "Mrs. Murkley used to teach there. It's a boarding school. I knew a boy who was sent there."

"And?" said Adélaïde.

"Well, I don't know," said Oliver. "He never said very much about it when he returned. He never said much of anything, really. He just sort of sat there, humming like an electric fan."

"Is that true?" Adélaïde asked Archer.

"I don't know," said Archer. "But we're not going to fail. And I don't understand why you've waited till now to say this."

"Because I never thought I'd actually have to do anything," said Oliver. "But it's all becoming much too real for me. I was only in this for friendship."

Adélaïde fiddled with an orange. It wasn't her original intention, but the more time she spent with these two, the more she liked them.

"I'm here for friendship, too," she said.

"Then we all agree," said Archer. "And who said anything about dying? I don't plan on dying."

"Nobody *plans* on dying," said Oliver.

"I nearly died," said Adélaïde.

"That's why you're not afraid," Oliver replied. "I've only had far-death experiences and I'd prefer to keep it that way."

"But that's not going to happen," said Archer. "Don't you see? My grandparents did great things together and I think we can, too. Beginning with finding them. This is your chance to become more than *just a Glub*."

"I like being just a Glub," said Oliver. "You two are the ones who like to court danger and swim with crocodiles and things like that. Me? I prefer to catch fireflies and see how many blueberries I can fit into my mouth. No one ever died from eating a blueberry."

"I'm sure someone did," said Adélaïde.

"But this is all happening for a reason," said Archer.

"Nothing happens for a reason," said Oliver. "Everywhere is chaos. Adélaïde was half-eaten by a crocodile. Your grandparents are stuck to the side of an iceberg. And my cat turned into a statue."

Archer and Adélaïde exchanged glances. Oliver sighed.

"Théo," he said. "He ate cement mix—I don't want to talk about it. What I'm trying to say is that I see this stuff everyday in my father's newspaper and there's no rhyme or reason to any of it. Terrible things just happen and you'd better get out of the way when they do."

"You can't always get out of the way," said Adélaïde.

"You need friends to pull you out of the way," said Archer.

Oliver stared at him. He couldn't argue with that. "But you're doing the opposite of pulling me out of the way."

"That's not true," said Archer. "If you don't come with us, you'll be alone with Mrs. Murkley."

Oliver turned to Adélaïde, who shrugged and popped an orange slice into her mouth. "You have a choice," she said.

"That's not a choice," said Oliver. "A choice is deciding whether to eat cake or ice."

"So choose cake," said Adélaïde.

Archer nodded. "Choose friendship."

The table fell silent. Oliver pushed his plate forward and

begrudgingly searched his pockets until he found the ad for survival kits that he'd torn from the deep-sea magazine. (He'd been carrying it ever since.)

"Can I see that card?" he asked Adélaïde. She gave it to him. It *was* the same shop. Oliver nodded and handed the card back to Archer.

"All right," he said. "But before I go anywhere, I need you both to promise me something."

"*Avec plaisir,*" said Adélaïde. "That means 'with pleasure.'"

Oliver didn't want a French lesson so he continued, speaking slowly. "If we find ourselves stuck to the side of an iceberg and I'm too cold to think, I need you to whisper in my ear the word *dig*."

"I promise to say *dig*," said Adélaïde, even though she thought this a strange request.

Archer nodded.

The sun was now a little higher in the sky. All three stared out across the rooftops in the direction of the ocean, much like Alexander the Great, sitting atop his elephant staring up at the Himalayas.

"So now what?" Adélaïde asked.

Archer held up his card.

"But it's Saturday," said Oliver.

Archer smiled. He knew exactly what day it was.

• Autumn Flowers •

Archer went to the edge of the roof and looked down into the gardens. Oliver and Adélaïde joined him and popped orange slices into their mouths.

"It's the autumn flower festival," said Archer.

Down below, all of the neighbors were busy making preparations for a day of garden tours, cider and cakes, and music. The Durnips' garden swelled with magnificent orange dahlia flowers while Mr. Malik showed his ruby hibiscuses to Mrs. Pemberton, who seemed much more impressed with her autumn roses.

"I don't think my father knows about this," said Adélaïde. "He'll be at the café all day. Not that it matters. Our flowers are dead. He didn't water anything."

"Mrs. Murkley's garden doesn't have any flowers," said Oliver. "They probably made a run for it during the night."

Archer and Adélaïde laughed. Then the three of them looked at the Glubs' infamous garden. "Your mother never expects much from us, Archer," said Oliver. "But I'm sure my mom will be hiding."

Mrs. Glub wouldn't be the only one hiding. Mr. Helmsley also went into hiding during these events. Archer didn't have to. He had been seven years old the one and only time his mother had asked him to help her. Shortly after she'd handed him the clippers and sent him to the garden, he had discovered a new box from his grandparents and was in such a rush to open it that he accidentally trimmed the tips off his mother's most treasured flowers: the Gerbertwolicks—a rare breed whose purple and red blooms can last three weeks (unless you cut them off with clippers). After that, Mrs. Helmsley instructed him to stay far away from her flowers.

"She'll be busy all day," Archer mumbled, scanning the gardens for his mother. She must be down there somewhere. She was. Mrs. Helmsley was in the Lepertons' garden, helping to perk up a dreary pot of chrysanthemums.

"You've watered them too much," Archer heard her say. Mrs. Leperton threw up her arms. "When you smother them like this, something bad is bound to happen!"

"This is our chance," said Archer. "We have to go now. We'll head to Strait of Magellan and see what we can find. And hopefully they'll know about ship schedules. If not, I'll figure something out."

One by the one, they climbed down the ladder to Oliver's room and dashed down the stairs, stopping on the third floor to grab a bus map. Mr. Glub was sitting in the living room. He lowered his newspaper when the trio spilled into the foyer. Archer, Oliver, and Adélaïde froze, their eyes fixed on

Mr. Glub. Mr. Glub smiled and raised his paper once more. Still, no one moved.

"I didn't see anything," Mr. Glub said from behind the paper. "If anyone asks, I didn't see a thing."

Archer looked at Adélaïde who looked at Oliver who looked back at Archer who shrugged and reached for the doorknob. They bent low as they passed beneath Archer's windows and the Lepertons' windows and once they were in the clear, took off down the sidewalk. Archer stopped after a few feet and spun around. Adélaïde, who was only operating on one good leg, mind you, could never run as quickly as the others. He went back and took her hand.

"You'd think I'd be better with it by now," she said.

"You'll figure it out," he replied, and together, they moved quickly down the sidewalk to join Oliver at the bus stop.

"How's your heart?" Adélaïde asked.

"Still beating," said Oliver.

CHAPTER

FOURTEEN

✦ Warehouse Ward ✦

Archer, Oliver, and Adélaïde sat on a bench in the shade of a tall stone wall, waiting for the bus. It was taking a while. Oliver opened the map and looked for Strait of Magellan. Adélaïde watched a pigeon perched atop a lamppost.

"That's in Barrow's Bay," said Oliver.

Archer knew nothing about it so Oliver explained. Barrow's Bay was a neighborhood on the easternmost edge of the city, near the ocean. There was a canal leading through it that arched up and cut Rosewood in two. Many people called Barrow's Bay "the Old Warehouse Ward" because it was mostly just that, once-beautiful warehouses turned crusty from the salty air. But whatever anyone called it, certain parts of Barrow's Bay were not the sort of places you should go wandering alone at night.

"We don't have to take the bus," said Oliver, tilting the map toward Archer. "We could walk through Rosewood Park. But there would still be a decent walk on the other side."

Archer would have preferred this. But he was afraid it would take too much time. His mother would only be occupied for so long.

"Let's take the bus," he said.

"We'll have to take two," said Oliver. He squinted at the map. "It almost looks like it's *inside* the canal."

A man with his pants tucked into knee-high boots strolled over and stood with his back to them.

"Why does he have an umbrella?" whispered Oliver.

"And rain boots?" whispered Archer.

"Storm's coming," said the man, without turning around.

Archer and Oliver looked up at the bright blue sky.

Finally, a Rosewood bus squealed to a halt. Oliver and Adélaïde followed the man up the steps and dropped their coins into the meter. Archer paused in the door. He glanced back at Willow Street, hoping his mother *would* be too busy in the gardens to check on him.

"On or off," said the bus driver. "Can't do both. You'll be ripped in half."

Archer turned and got on the bus. "Sorry," he said, and dropped his coins into the meter.

"Back here!" shouted Oliver from the rear of the bus. Adélaïde threw up her hand. Archer walked past the stares of strangers and took a seat next to Adélaïde.

• On the Fritz •

Rosewood buses, like most city buses, are often filled with odd individuals, and it's best to mind your business while riding one. But it's difficult to stop yourself from looking at each person and wondering about their oddities. So long as they don't catch you staring, this is a perfectly fine thing to do, and Archer was doing just that as the bus sped off down the street. An old lady was eating a bag of lemon drops that made her lips pucker. This made Archer wonder. If she put the lot in her mouth at once, would her entire face pucker?

Oliver reached up to crack open a window, but the additional breeze wasn't enough to clear the dank air.

"It smells like a dog in here," he said.

"Because there *is* a dog in here," replied Adélaïde.

Indeed, seated directly across from them was an all too proper-looking gentleman with a muddy silver spoon wedged into his blazer pocket, and seated next to him was a beagle with muddy paws. Adélaïde stood up to scratch the creature's head.

Lemon

"What's his name?" she asked.

"Fritz," the man replied. "I always name them Fritz."

"He's a nice dog. How old is he?"

"Three years and he's not a nice dog." The man gave the beagle a stern look. The beagle licked its snout. "Doesn't know how to behave, this one. I do to him today what I should have done to him two years ago."

"What should you have done to him two years ago?" Archer asked.

"We're on our way to the pound," he said. "They'll put him down."

Adélaïde straightened. "That's awful," she said. "You can't do that!"

The man coughed into a handkerchief, taken aback. "I can and I will," he replied.

Adélaïde was appalled. And the worst part about it was Fritz looked perfectly happy to be out and about. But only because he didn't know his life was about to take a turn for the worse. She looked at Oliver, who shrugged.

"It's better than eating cement mix," he said.

One stop later, when the bus driver shouted, "Thistlery Street," the man stood up.

"Wait," said Adélaïde. "Let me have him."

The man coughed into his handkerchief a second time and

tried to leave, but Adélaïde placed herself in front of him.

"Trust me," he said. "You don't want this dog. Now out of my way!"

"What difference does it make?" Adélaïde said, sticking out her hand. "You won't have to worry about him anymore."

The man stared at Adélaïde, then down at Fritz. The bus driver shifted in his seat.

"Get off or sit down!" he shouted.

The man took one last look at Adélaïde before dropping the leash into her hand and stepping off the bus.

Oliver smacked Archer. "She's crazy!" he said.

"So why are you hitting *me*?" said Archer, rubbing his arm.

Adélaïde sat down and knocked her shoulder against Oliver's. "You're the one who just said you didn't want to die in a bowl of soup. Why should Fritz?"

"I don't think that's how they do it," Oliver grumbled.

Adélaïde placed Fritz on her lap and rubbed his head. They transferred to the next bus two stops later and continued on to Barrow's Bay.

"What exactly are we getting?" asked Oliver.

"I'm not sure," said Adélaïde.

Oliver eyed her with a growing suspicion. For everything she said she'd done, she didn't know very much about anything.

"I'm not certain either," said Archer, flipping through his

notebook. "I think it's best if first we see what they have. Then we can decide what we need. But we can't take much."

Outside the bus windows, the buildings were growing taller and taller, as were their shadows. Suddenly, the bus stopped short. Adélaïde grabbed Fritz, who nearly flipped off her lap. The driver shouted, "Turntail Way."

Oliver stood up. "This is us," he said.

The trio stepped off the bus and into the shadows of giant warehouses, looming high over their heads. One end of Turntail Way led to more warehouses and shadows. Down the opposite way, Archer saw a sunny opening.

"Let's go that way," he said.

• In a Moldy Sort of Way •

Archer, Oliver, and Adélaïde stepped out from the warehouse shadows and found themselves staring out at the Rosewood Canal. Crooked trees lined the towpath and threw shadows on small wooden boats drifting in the greenish water. They weren't very far from Willow Street but that's not what it felt like. Even the air was different. The ocean was near, and they could feel the salt sticking to their cheeks as they followed down a stone stairway to the canal and stood just a few inches above the water.

"It's beautiful," said Adélaïde.

"In a moldy sort of way," agreed Oliver.

Archer was quiet. He didn't know such places existed in Rosewood. And seeing this canal stretching far in both directions made him wonder what else he didn't know about.

A few people flitted this way and that. Archer tried to stop a man to ask for directions, but the man ignored him. Oliver consulted his map, then looked south to where the canal curved left and widened. In the very center of the water was a narrow island, no more than a hundred yards long and half as wide as that. The buildings that lined this strip appeared to rise straight up out of the greenish water.

"I think it's there," said Oliver. "That's why it looked like it was inside the canal."

They set off down the walkway, past small bridges and doorways that looked like secret entrances to shops above the canal's wall. They crossed a bridge that stretched to the narrow island and fell silent when they reached the other side. The buildings here were much older than those on Willow Street, or at least they looked much older, and cutting down the center of the island was a cobbled street, all in shadow except where bits of sunlight pierced the cracks between the buildings. A sign above their heads read "Barrow's Strip."

"I don't want to go down there," said Oliver.

Adélaïde agreed. Fritz was too busy sniffing a rotten fish

to have an opinion either way. Archer wasn't eager either, but he convinced them to follow him. Oliver and Adélaïde did so with twitching eyes. They weren't certain what sort of shops these were or what sort of customers frequented them, but they were certain few eleven-year-olds would spend time in such a place.

"I feel like we're being watched," Oliver whispered.

"We are being watched," Adélaïde replied, nodding at hazy silhouettes in dusty shop windows.

Archer stopped and looked up at the façade of a once-majestic building.

"That's it?" said Oliver. "That can't be it."

"It looks a little—*dusty*," said Adélaïde.

The building was four stories high and seemed to stare down at them as they stared up at it. Archer looked at his card. The address was correct. And he could just make out the words *Strait of Magellan* at the top of the building. This was it. But it wasn't what he had imagined.

"Well," he said, placing the card back in his pocket. "I guess we'll see." He pushed hard against the heavy door and disappeared inside.

Oliver and Adélaïde hesitated.

"Ladies and children first," said Oliver.

Adélaïde smiled and curtsied, which somehow turned into

a fancy spin, and before Oliver knew what was happening, she was behind him, grabbing tight to his shoulders and pushing him toward the door.

"Children should always go before ladies," she said.

• Not So Strait of Magellan •

Adélaïde and Oliver nearly bumped into Archer. They couldn't see a thing, but their noses flared with the scent of crusted salt spray. Once their eyes adjusted to the dimly lit shop, they could see it was packed with all sorts of equipment. Wooden racks stretched every which way, piled high with goggles and helmets and ropes and oxygen tanks and still more things they didn't know the purposes of. Adélaïde was right. Everything was covered in a healthy bit of dust.

"I don't think I'd trust any of this stuff," said Oliver.

"And why not?" came an unkind voice from the back room.

A chair on wheels squeaked into the doorway and the man sitting on it leaned back to get a look at them. Archer squinted, but a window behind the chair made this man a dark silhouette.

"This is not a chocolate shop," the man said. "You'll find nothing sweet in this salty place."

"We need equipment," said Archer.

"We're going on a journey," said Adélaïde.

"Is there a chocolate shop nearby?" asked Oliver.

The man left the squeaky chair. He leaned against a wooden counter and fished something from his teeth while glancing them over. Unlike the name of his shop, this man looked very crooked.

"You'll be paying for anything that dog breaks," he said, glaring at Adélaïde with deep-set deep blue eyes.

"He didn't break anything," she replied, pulling Fritz tight.

"Not yet he hasn't," the man grumbled. "Aren't you all a little *young* to be going anywhere?"

"We're older than we look," said Archer. "I think you knew my grandparents. Grandma and Grandpa Helmsley."

"You probably didn't call them 'Grandma' and 'Grandpa,' though," Oliver clarified.

The man didn't have eyebrows in the traditional sense, but if he did, they would have gone up after hearing this.

"Which would make you Archer Helmsley?" he asked.

Adélaïde and Oliver exchanged glances. Archer wasn't comfortable with this man knowing his name either.

"They mentioned you a number of times," the man said, and pressed his tongue into his sunken cheek. "There hasn't been any news on the iceberg, I hope?"

Archer wasn't sure why he put it like that, but no, there hadn't been any news on the iceberg. "That's why we're here," he explained. "We're going to find them."

At that, the crooked man erupted with laughter and couldn't stop.

"It's not funny," said Adélaïde. "We're serious."

"Yes, my dear." Laughter. "You are *quite* the little peg-legged pirate, aren't you?"

Oliver pushed back his shoulders and said, "At least she has eyebrows!"

The man stopped laughing. Oliver wished he'd remained silent. Adélaïde turned to Archer, who was looking a little smaller than usual.

"We don't need his help," she said. "Let's just find what we need and get out of this creepy place."

"Take your time," said the crooked man, smiling.

While Adélaïde and Archer disappeared farther into the store, Oliver lingered at the counter. He removed the ad for survival kits and politely asked the crooked man where he might find them.

"You'd better watch that tongue of yours," the man replied, snatching the paper from Oliver's hand. "Or I just might cut it out of your head."

Oliver leaned back. That didn't sound like an empty threat.

This man made Mrs. Murkley look like a sugar plum fairy.

"Fourth floor," said the crooked man, pointing up.

Oliver tilted his head. The entire center of the store was hollow. He could see different landings with railings, circling up four flights.

"Best watch yourself up there," the crooked man said. "That's a long way to fall."

Archer and Adélaïde took their time wandering the aisles inspecting odd devices. Because they didn't know what they needed, their decisions came down to whether or not they knew what the equipment did and whether or not they could easily carry it. They selected rope and hooks, an ice pick, and Adélaïde found a small shovel for Oliver. Archer realized he had seen a number of the odd devices in his house, and if there was room, they could take them from home. This led Archer to think about his grandparents' trunks. He told Adélaïde about them as they climbed the stairs to the second floor, and both agreed it would be a good idea if they could find them as there might be things inside that they could use.

Archer and Adélaïde leaned against the second-floor railing. Fritz stuck his head between the spindles and tried desperately to lick the salt from the air.

"Is your father going to be angry when you bring a dog home?" Archer asked.

"No," said Adélaide. "He won't care."

"If I did something like that I think my mother would—" Archer stopped. He caught a strong whiff of gasoline and someone tapped his shoulder. He spun around. It was the Eye Patch.

✦ The Society ✦

"*Oh*—hello," said Archer.

"I thought that was you, Archer Helmsley," the Eye Patch replied.

Adélaïde bit her lip, but she was growing used to the idea that there were many odd strangers who knew Archer by name. The Eye Patch put his hand on Archer's shoulder.

"I was wondering if I might ever see you again," he said. "And I'm glad I have. But I must ask what you're doing in this place? Never thought I'd see you in here."

Archer didn't want to be laughed at again so he said they were walking by and stopped to have a look.

"Do you work here?" he added.

The Eye Patch didn't. "I'm only in Rosewood a short while—just here to pick up a few things."

Adélaïde ran her finger over the dusty railing and made a squiggle while watching these two from the corner of her eye.

"You knew my grandparents, didn't you?" Archer asked.

"Very well," said the Eye Patch. "Wonderful people. Ralph and Rachel were loved by many in our community."

"And you do still think they're alive, don't you?"

"I have no reason to," the Eye Patch admitted. "But I do."

"Don't lie to the boy!" shouted the crooked man, peering up from the first floor. "They're dead—frozen solid. And I'm one of the few who can drink to that! *Waiter, bring me two Helmsleys on the rocks!*"

Adélaïde watched the crooked man dance a queer jig behind the counter. The Eye Patch leaned forward and lowered his voice so that only they could hear.

"Don't pay him any mind," he said. "It's in his interest *financially* that Ralph and Rachel remain missing."

"Financially?" asked Archer.

The Eye Patch nodded. "As you can imagine, there were lots of bets at the Society after the iceberg."

Archer couldn't imagine. "Bets about what? And what Society?"

"You must know about the Society," said the Eye Patch, straightening. Archer didn't. "But your grandfather was the president! And a highly respected one at that. Well, not by everyone, of course. There are a number of factions at the Society."

Archer was hopelessly confused and after saying as much, the Eye Patch explained.

The Society was an organization for individuals like himself and Archer's grandparents. It was also in Barrow's Bay, not far from where they were now, in fact, and it had been there for nearly two hundred years. A number of members lived there, renting rooms on the top floors, while others stayed for shorter periods. This was where the Eye Patch stayed whenever he was in Rosewood.

"It's a marvelous place," he said with a glittering eye. "Filled with fascinating characters. But I doubt your Willow Street has seen many of them. I attracted lots of stares while delivering those trunks—felt terrible about that, by the way. Never forgot your expression when you opened that door. Thought you might slam it in my face!"

The Eye Patch went on to explain that disappearances were not uncommon in their community. And when such things did happen, many bets were placed on whether or not those who disappeared would someday reappear.

"Are you saying you bet against my grandparents being alive?" Archer asked, still trying to digest all of this.

"Of course not!" said the Eye Patch. "Not me. I told you when we first met, I put my bets on them being alive."

He nodded toward the crooked man.

"I'm sorry to tell you that pelican of a man took the opposite stance and made heaps of money doing so—him, Birthwhistle, and the rest of their flock did. Everyone waits a year to see what happens, so they've long since collected their money. Of course, if we're right, if Ralph and Rachel return, they'll have a pretty penny to cough up and I'll smoke my pipe to that!"

The crooked man was stretching with his arms pressed tight to his spine. Archer thought he was more crooked than ever.

"But enough with all that," said the Eye Patch, turning his eye to Adélaïde. "Who's your friend?"

Archer looked at her. She nodded. "This is Adélaïde," he said. "She's French and was half-eaten by a crocodile. And that's Fritz. He almost died, too. I have another friend named Oliver. He's around here somewhere."

"If you don't mind me asking," said Adélaïde, now that they'd been introduced. "What exactly happened to your eye?"

The man rubbed a greasy finger against the patch and smiled. "I'm afraid it's not half the story your crocodile is," he said. "Just a deck winch malfunction in rough seas. But tell me, where was this croc—"

"Rough seas," said Archer. "Does that mean you have a ship?"

The Eye Patch nodded proudly. "I'm the captain of one, in fact."

Archer and Adélaïde were thinking the same thing. *The glass eye?*

"Is your ship in Rosewood Port?" Archer asked.

"She certainly is," the Eye Patch replied. "I've had that ship for—"

"You wouldn't be going to Antarctica any time soon, would you?" Adélaïde asked.

"Can't say I am—don't go in for those climates. I always say, if it's too—"

"But do you know ship schedules?" Archer asked. "When they're leaving and where they're going?"

"I don't," said the Eye Patch. He pointed at the crooked man. "But he does. Follow me!"

Archer and Adélaïde excitedly followed the Eye Patch down the stairs and back to the front counter. The Eye Patch asked to see the docking schedule, but had to insist before the crooked man dropped a massive book on the counter. He opened it to the most recent page and spun the book toward

Archer in a cloud of dust. Archer ran his finger over the list. *Antarctica.* There was only one ship.

"The *Tory Beacon* is a research vessel," said the Eye Patch, leaning over Archer's shoulder. "Leaves in nine days. Dock E7."

Archer wrote this down in his notebook.

"Nine days," he said. "That's October sixth—the Monday after next. Isn't there something on October sixth?"

"That's the museum trip," said Oliver, waddling up behind them and dropping a large box labeled "Survival Kit" on the counter. He was dusty and breathing heavily. "That's when we go to the Rosewood Museum."

"And you must be Oliver?" said the Eye Patch with a grin.

Oliver glanced at the greasy man and then at Archer.

"Are we in danger?" he asked.

"No," said Adélaïde.

"Nine days?" repeated Archer. "I'm not sure we'll be ready in nine days."

The Eye Patch leaned against the counter. "What's this you're looking to be ready for?" he asked casually.

They didn't hear him.

"We'll be fine," said Adélaïde.

"But we still have a few things to do," said Archer.

The Eye-Patch tapped Oliver's box. "*Survival kit?*"

"Nine days is plenty," said Adélaïde.

"It'll have to be," said Archer.

"HOLD IT!" shouted the Eye Patch. All three of them jumped. "Sorry—but why did you want to know about ships going to Antarctica?"

"Because that's where they're going," said the crooked man with a crooked smile.

The Eye Patch shook his head. "You can't go to Antarctica."

"They'll never get inside Rosewood Port," the crooked man replied.

"I think we will," said Adélaïde.

"We're small enough," said Oliver with a sigh.

The crooked man shut the book. Oliver sneezed.

"I don't care where you go," he said. "I only care to know how you plan to pay for all of this."

Archer handed the crooked man his card. "There's an account number there," he said. "You can charge all of it to that."

"If it doesn't say your name, you can't use it."

"But I'm a Helmsley."

"And how do I know that?"

"You're the one who knew him before he said anything," said Adélaïde.

"He knows me," said Archer, pointing to the Eye Patch, who nodded.

"I've been to the house on Willow Street. He's a Helmsley. But he's not going to Antarctica."

"This account has been inactive for two years," said the crooked man. "Doubt there's any money in it."

"There's always money in the Helmsleys' accounts," said the Eye Patch stiffly.

The crooked man grumbled and headed to the back room. The Eye Patch stood silently staring at Archer. When the crooked man returned, he piled the items into bags. Archer handed one to Oliver and one to Adélaïde and they made for the exit, ignoring the crooked man's snide farewell. The Eye Patch followed them to the door.

"You can't go to Antarctica," he said.

Archer liked the Eye Patch, but he was tired of hearing this. "Maybe not," he replied. "But I have to try. And I hope I'll see you again."

"It was nice meeting you," said Adélaïde, following Oliver outside.

Archer paused. "Did you take my grandparents to Antarctica?" he asked.

The Eye Patch didn't.

"Then why did you deliver their trunks?"

"They were in storage at the Society," he replied. "I happened upon them and volunteered to take them to Willow Street."

"Yes," said Archer. "But why were they sent to the Society in the first place? Why weren't they sent home?"

The Eye Patch scratched his neck and seemed confused. "The Society was their home," he said. "They'd been renting a few rooms there for nine years or so. Up until the iceberg, of course."

Archer shook his head. That couldn't be right. "They were never in Rosewood," he said. "They'd been traveling ever since I was born."

"No one travels for nine years straight! Especially at their age. No, Ralph and Rachel were at the Society quite often."

• Barrow's Bay All Along •

Oliver and Adélaïde sat on the edge of the canal with their bare feet submerged in the green speckled water. Fritz fell asleep on the warm cobblestones. A small wooden boat drifted by. Adélaïde let her wooden leg bob to the surface.

"Aren't you worried it'll get waterlogged?" Oliver asked.

"No," she replied. "I can always get a new one."

They were both watching Archer, who was skipping stones not far away. He'd told them everything he learned from the Eye Patch, but it still hadn't sunk in. It all made sense while making no sense at all.

Of course his grandparents didn't travel for nine years

without ever once coming home. That was simply what his parents wanted him to believe. His mother probably asked them to leave Helmsley House after he was born. She didn't want them around him. The house was already too much for her. So they moved into the Society.

Then there were the boxes. His grandparents must have left those on the doorstep themselves when they returned from trips. That's why he was told to keep them a secret. That's why his mother looked confused when she found them. She must have thought they were secretly visiting him. And while he could understand why his mother would keep their whereabouts a secret, he didn't understand why his father had.

Archer skipped his last stone, removed his shoes and socks, and joined the others. The water was cool. The green specks dotted his feet.

"They were living in Barrow's Bay all along," he said.

"You don't know why they didn't tell you," said Adélaïde thoughtfully. "I don't think you should assume anything."

"But it's obvious," said Oliver. "His mother didn't want him to meet them."

"Obvious is not always right," said Adélaïde.

"What I don't understand," said Archer, "is why they left the house in the first place. Why let me in if it meant they would move out?"

"I think they wanted you to grow up there," said Adélaïde. "That would have made their decision easy and they were probably glad to do it. You'd be different if you grew up in a house without a polar bear."

Archer couldn't help but smile at this. He also never would have met Oliver and Adélaïde.

"I just don't—" Archer stopped. A prickly sensation came over him.

"You just don't what?" said Oliver.

"I think I've *met* him," said Archer.

"What do you mean?" Adélaïde asked.

It took Archer a moment, but he explained the story of the scraggly man from the dinner party—the man who stumbled as he walked. And while he couldn't remember what that man looked like, he never forgot what that man told him: "*You're a Helmsley. And being a Helmsley means something.*"

"But it couldn't have been him," said Oliver. "Not if that man could barely walk."

"Anyone could pretend to do that," said Adélaïde.

"It *was* him," said Archer. "I'm sure it was. And after that, the boxes began arriving."

Archer had always been certain he would know exactly who his grandfather was, but the one time he met him, he didn't even know it. He plucked a piece of grass from a crack in the cobblestones and tossed it into the water.

"What do you want to do?" Adélaïde asked.

Archer wanted to see the Society. He wanted to see where his grandparents lived. He wanted to see the world that was kept secret from him. The world the Eye Patch called "marvelous." But making sure they were on that ship mattered most. None of this changed the fact that Ralph and Rachel were still stuck on an iceberg.

"They gave up their house for me," he said. "We have to get on that ship."

"We will," assured Adélaïde.

"I don't want to take any chances," he replied. "We should go to Rosewood Port. It can't be very far. We need to see exactly what we'll be dealing with."

So that's what they did. They dried their feet, slipped into their shoes, and followed the canal, which, according to Oliver's map, would lead them to the port. It was a pleasant walk and Archer's mood lightened as they climbed another stone stairway and entered Rosewood Port.

• Stop Those Turtles •

Seagulls drifted with the wind. The empty streets of Barrow's Bay were replaced with great crowds. The shimmering ocean stretched out before them and the port was like a giant mouth trying to drink it. To the right were smaller ships and to the left were much larger ones. At the very center was a long stone building with arched entrances. Adélaïde pointed out what she could remember, but she had arrived at night and everything always looks different at night.

"We can't go inside," she said. "They won't let you onto the docks without a ticket and we don't have any."

There was a second way onto the docks—where the cargo was brought on carts and trucks to be loaded onto ships. It was a narrow gate with a small guard booth on one side. They moved in to take a closer look. At most, the guard inside the booth looked like he was qualified to stop a turtle, but only if he put his mind to it. Still, there was no way to get past without his noticing.

"That's it," said Archer. "That's how we'll get inside."

"But he'll see us," said Oliver.

"He must take breaks," said Adélaïde.

"Maybe," said Oliver. "But we won't know that for sure. We can't just walk up and ask when he won't be there."

To their surprise, that was precisely what Adélaïde was going to do. She stuck her hand into Oliver's pocket and removed half a croissant.

"*How did you*—I was going to eat that!" Oliver cried, but

Adélaïde ignored him and slowly approach the booth with Fritz.

Once she was close enough, she bent down and unleashed the beagle. She flashed the croissant in front of his nose and lobbed it. The croissant bounced off the booth's glass window. The guard looked up. Fritz took off after it. The guard rushed out and scooped him up just as Adélaïde hurried over.

"I guess he can stop more than a turtle," whispered Oliver.

"Merci, Monsieur!" said Adélaïde. *"Parlez-vous Français?"*

"I don't understand a word you're saying," the guard replied, at the same moment noticing Archer and Oliver. "You can't be over here. None of you are supposed to be over here!"

"Oh," said Adélaïde. "I'm sorry. We're from France. We didn't know." She turned to Archer and Oliver, who picked up on her cue and began looking around the port with confused expressions, pointing to this and that.

"Thank you for saving him, by the way," she said, facing the guard once more. "He can't swim very well."

"This belongs to you?" the guard asked.

"He," said Adélaïde. "His name is Fritz. He escaped while we were touring the port. It's quite lovely. Except for your booth. That looks rather small. Do you sit in there all day long?"

"I do," he said slowly.

"Well, I'm sorry to hear that. You must get terribly cramped in there. Do they let you take breaks?"

Archer and Oliver shook their heads, certain the guard would see right through this. She was being too obvious. If they were in his shoes, they would know she was lying. But they were amazed to see the guard's expression soften. And still more amazed to see that he appreciated her concern.

"It's not so terrible as that," he said. "I usually get to stretch the legs and grab a coffee every hour or so."

"Oh, that's very good," she replied. "I'm glad to hear it."

The guard handed Fritz to Adélaïde and his look stiffened once more.

"Now I must ask the three of you to leave," he said, and squeezed himself back into the booth.

Adélaïde thanked him and walked back to Archer and Oliver. They stared. Adélaïde pretended not to notice.

"Gets coffee every hour or so," she said with a shrug, now unable to hold back a smile. Archer shook his head.

"You scare me sometimes," said Oliver.

Adélaïde giggled and threw her arms around both their shoulders.

"But I'm on *your* side," she said.

"I hope so."

They gathered their bags and followed the canal back to Turntail Way, boarded one Rosewood bus and then another. And when the driver shouted, "Willow Street," they stepped off with their equipment, a departure date, and a beagle named Fritz.

CHAPTER FIFTEEN

✦ Permission to Sneak ✦

Archer struggled against telling his parents everything he discovered in Barrow's Bay. He had more questions than the Eye Patch had answers, but he couldn't say a word. If he did, they would know he'd left the house and spoken to someone he shouldn't have. So Archer kept his mouth shut and when Monday rolled around, he had many other things on his mind. The ship to Antarctica would be leaving in one week. They'd done their research and their equipment and winter clothes were packed into bags, but they still had to figure out how they were going to get to the port. They met in the reading room to work out the remaining details.

"The ship leaves the same day as the museum trip," Oliver said, sounding annoyed because Adélaïde was dominating him on the checkers board.

Archer was lying on the couch with his notebook. "There's no reason to come to school that day," he said. "We'll sneak out through your house and head straight to the port."

Adélaïde disagreed. "We'll need *time* to get to Rosewood Port before anyone realizes we're gone," she said. "If we don't show up for school, Mrs. Murkley will call our parents. We won't make it."

"But they won't know where we're going," said Oliver.

This was true, but Archer didn't want to chance it. They would escape during the museum trip and that would hopefully allow for enough time to get to Rosewood Port. But this meant they would have to cut down on what they were bringing.

"It'll look suspicious if our bags are too big," Archer said. "We'll bring one change of clothes and the equipment, but nothing more."

Oliver threw up his hands. Adélaïde quadruple-jumped him for the win. He left the checkers board and joined Archer on the couch.

"I'm surprised that's even an option," he said. "I didn't think your mother would let you go to the museum."

Archer was silent.

"She did sign the slip, didn't she?" Adélaïde asked.

Archer closed his eyes. He'd forgotten about the permission slip.

"I'll ask her tonight," he said.

But that night during dinner, Mrs. Helmsley was in a foul mood.

"These flower festivals have taken a terrible turn," she said. "Mrs. Murkley's garden was completely sterile, not a speck of color. And the Glubs', well, that was no surprise. But the new people, what's their name?"

"The Belmonts," said Mr. Helmsley.

"Yes, well, I've seen graveyard flowers with more life."

The permission slip stayed in Archer's pocket. Now was not a good time to ask. He wanted to wait till his mother was in a better mood, but by Thursday, she was *still* annoyed. Archer was running out of time. He removed the permission slip and made his pitch.

"That's not going to happen," Mrs. Helmsley said.

"It's only a school trip," said Mr. Helmsley. "I don't see why not."

"Well I do," she replied. "And it's a terrible idea."

Archer was desperate. "Oliver is going," he said.

"What the Glubs do with Oliver is none of my business," his mother replied. "Besides, Oliver doesn't have your *tendencies*."

"You mean Oliver isn't locked inside his house!" he said, and stormed out of the dining room, afraid he might say something else he shouldn't. If his mother wouldn't sign the slip, he would find another way.

• Wild Animals •

"But there isn't another way," said Oliver the next day at the Button Factory. "We've already gone through this."

Adélaïde left Miss Whitewood's desk and sat down on the rug.

"I was thinking we should look for those trunks on Saturday and—" She stopped when she saw Archer's and Oliver's expressions. "What's going on?"

Archer handed her the unsigned slip.

"They wouldn't do it," said Oliver.

Adélaïde and Oliver looked at each other. No one said anything. Then a pen clicked.

"What are their names?" she asked, pretending to read the paper.

"You can't do that," said Oliver.

Adélaïde stood up and wedged herself between them on the couch.

"Sometimes you have to do what you want even when others think you're crazy."

Oliver sighed. She had it backward. "Sometimes you have to do what you think is crazy because it's what others want."

"We have to finish!" Adélaïde insisted. "Otherwise this has all been a waste of time."

Archer hesitated. Was it not enough that he would be sneaking out of his house and boarding a ship to Antarctica? Was he also going to add forging his parents' signatures to his list of infringements?

"If we get caught sneaking aboard a ship to Antarctica, do you really think the permission slip will make it any worse?" said Adélaïde.

She was right. It wouldn't make any difference. And they had done too much to turn back now, so he told her his parents' names and she wrote them in neat cursive.

"You'll turn this in after lunch," she said. "Mrs. Murkley won't know the difference." And that was that.

"Now," she continued without second thoughts. "I really think we should look for those trunks. The last place your grandparents were was Antarctica. There *must* be something in there. But I can't do it tonight. I promised to help my father at the café. Amaury hasn't arrived yet. We can do it tomorrow."

"Wait," said Oliver. "I think you're both overlooking something important. Do you really think it's going to be so simple to slip away in the museum without her noticing?

This is Mrs. Murkley we're talking about. You know"—Oliver puffed out his cheeks, lowered his brow, and beat his fists against his chest—"that Mrs. Murkley."

Archer and Adélaïde giggled.

"We'll have to sneak away one by one," said Archer.

He would go first, followed by Adélaïde, and Oliver would bring up the rear. They would meet next to Tappenkuse and from there, make for the back exit and slip out into Rosewood Park.

"But what if she notices the two of you are missing before I can get away?" said Oliver. "I'll need a good excuse."

"Tell her we're in the bathroom," said Archer.

Oliver narrowed his eyes. "I said a *good* excuse. And what if she comes looking for you? Or all of us?"

"We mustn't be ourselves," said Adélaïde.

"Who are we supposed to be?" said Oliver. "Alice, Charlie, and Molly?"

"*Masks*," she clarified. "We should make masks to cover our faces."

"That won't fool her."

"It will from a distance."

"Animal masks," said Archer. "The museum is filled with animals."

Adélaïde said she would be a lion. Archer chose a badger.

Oliver, still thinking this somewhat pointless, didn't have a preference, so Adélaïde said he would be a gazelle.

"They're very fast and that's what you'll need to be."

On Saturday afternoon, Oliver and Adélaïde climbed down the ladder to Archer's room, and they spent a short while making masks. When they finished, they took them up to the rooftop, stood side-by-side, and slipped them on. Out of nowhere, and at the top of her lungs, Adélaïde let out a "*ROAR!*" It was perfectly primal and made the other two laugh. Archer wasn't sure what sound a badger made, but his "*Howl!*" didn't sound terribly out of place. Oliver was equally uncertain about the gazelle, so he simply cried, "*Gazelle, gazelle!*" over and over in short, staccato tones like a chirping bird.

Adélaïde pushed up her mask. "The trunks?" she asked.

Archer nodded. "But you'll have to do as I say down there. If my mother catches us, it will ruin everything."

• Behind Cellar Doors •

Neither Adélaïde nor Oliver had been inside the lower rooms of Helmsley House before, and they kept stopping to stare at all of the artifacts and animals. Archer had to continually nudge them along. When they finally reached the top of the main stair, Archer told them to wait and he slowly crept down. The main stair ended between a doorway to the dining room and a doorway to a sitting room. He carefully stuck his head around the corner. Mrs. Helmsley was in the sitting room reading a book. They couldn't go all the way down, not without being seen.

"We'll have to go over the side," he whispered.

Archer went first, hoisting himself over the banister and onto a chair next to the cellar door. Oliver followed and then Adélaïde, but Adélaïde lost her balance and toppled headfirst toward the badger. Archer and Oliver grabbed her, but not before she let out a soft yelp.

"Archer?" Mrs. Helmsley called.

Archer froze. Oliver glanced over his shoulder. They were holding the top half of Adélaïde. Her legs were on the chair and her face was up against the badger's.

"She's pretty," whispered the badger.

"Shhh," shushed Archer.

"Who are you shushing?" whispered Oliver.

"Is that you, Archer?!" called Mrs. Helmsley.

A book shut. Footsteps approached the stairs. Archer and Oliver reeled. They quickly lowered Adélaïde and dove for the cellar door, shutting it just as Mrs. Helmsley entered the hall.

Archer motioned for them to continue down the cellar

stairs, but it was pitch-black and the others couldn't see him. He felt along the wall for the shelf, and when he found it, he grabbed a flashlight and handed two more to Oliver and Adélaïde. At the bottom of the stairs, they shined their lights all around the cellar. It was a large, damp, stony vault filled with crates and creatures and strange machines. Massive piles surrounded stone supports that stretched up from the ground and arched at the ceiling. It was like a dustier version of the upstairs.

"It's creepy," whispered Oliver. "And it smells like old wet newspapers down here."

"Old wet newspapers?" questioned Adélaïde.

Oliver shrugged. "A pipe burst in our house once and flooded my father's office."

"It just smells old," she said.

"It is old," whispered Archer. "All of this belonged to my grandparents."

Oliver went to hit the light switch. Archer stopped him.

"She'll see the lights under the door," he said.

"The flashlights are fine," whispered Adélaïde. "But if she does come down, there are plenty of places to hide."

"That's why I'm not sure if we'll find the trunks," said Archer.

They decided to split up, and wove through the scattered

stacks and piles. They searched with no success for half an hour. Archer's flashlight flickered over a large black metal bowl. It was dented all around, with three stubby legs at the bottom. After inspecting it, he had an idea and whispered to Oliver, who spun around and blinded him with the light.

"Sorry," he said. "What's going on?"

Archer pointed his light at the black metal bowl. Oliver nodded, but wasn't sure why Archer was pointing to it.

"It's nice," Oliver said.

"We can use it to make a fire," said Archer.

"Metal doesn't burn."

"That's the point."

Archer said it would be a good idea if they skipped a comfortable night of sleeping in beds and slept on the rooftop for practice. Oliver liked the idea more than Archer, but only because he was thinking about marshmallows.

"And we'll make a fire in this," said Archer.

Oliver looked over his shoulder at Adélaïde. She was digging against the far wall.

"There's something I've wanted to ask you about her," he whispered. "Do you still ever think she's lying? She doesn't seem to know very much. And you saw how easily she duped that guard. What if she's duping us?"

Archer shook his head. "She wouldn't do that," he said.

Adélaïde flashed her light at them. "Back here!" she whispered.

Adélaïde had discovered there was more to the wall than it appeared. Two doors with stained-glass inserts were covering a hole five feet high and four feet across.

"They might be in here," she whispered.

Archer handed Oliver his flashlight and helped Adélaïde slide one door over and then the second. The alcove went farther back than they could see, but sure enough, sitting just inside were all four scarlet trunks. And not only the trunks. The journals and packages tied with red string were sitting on top.

"You found them," whispered Archer.

"They're quite beautiful," she replied.

Oliver held all three flashlights, shining them over their heads as Archer and Adélaïde quietly dragged the trunks out of the damp alcove.

"Your mother really didn't want you to find those," said Oliver.

"I don't think she made the hole," said Adélaïde.

"Just good use of it," said Archer.

They knelt before separate trunks and lifted the latches. Archer's trunk was filled with his grandfather's belongings—an old sweater, a dirty pair of boots, and a tin of milk candies that should have been eaten long ago.

Adélaïde removed a gold medallion, depicting a woman with three heads, and a stack of photos from her trunk. "They've been everywhere," she said, flipping through the photos. She paused at one of young Ralph Helmsley, sitting in a comfortable chair with a crooked smile and grease-stained cheeks. "You look like him," she said, and handed it to Archer.

Archer studied the photo. He *did* look like his grandfather. He slipped it into his pocket.

Oliver lifted a wooden case from his trunk. Inside were corked bottles containing colorful powders and liquids. He removed one filled with a dark blue dust and pink specks.

"What do you suppose this does?" he asked, showing it to Adélaïde.

"Taste it and find out," she replied.

"Théo ate a basement mixture he didn't understand," said Oliver. "I'm not doing the same."

They were all disappointed after opening the fourth and final trunk. They were expecting to find equipment or something they could use, but aside from personal belongings, all of the trunks had been mostly filled with items that would be as useful as a glass eye. Archer did, however, find a leather satchel full of odd metal tools.

"These will be useful," he said.

"But we're trying to rescue your grandparents," said Oliver. "Not carve the iceberg into a swan."

Archer's grin quickly vanished. Footsteps sounded overhead. It was nearing dinnertime and they must be somewhere below the kitchen.

"We should go," he said.

Oliver and Adélaïde piled everything back inside the trunks while Archer searched the boxes. He found the jade elephant house and dropped it into his pocket along with the photograph of his grandfather.

"They would've hated this," said Archer, as they pushed the trunks back into the alcove and slid the doors into place. "Those trunks don't belong in a hole in the wall."

Oliver and Adélaïde agreed, but for now, that's where they would stay. They dusted themselves off and stepped quietly back to the foot of the stairs.

"Do you have sleeping bags?" Archer asked.

Oliver did. Adélaïde didn't.

"I'll find an extra one for you," he said.

"Why do we need sleeping bags?"

"We're camping on the roof," said Oliver.

Archer crept up the steps and poked his head out from the cellar door. Mrs. Helmsley was in the kitchen. He motioned and Oliver and Adélaïde hurried up the stairs.

✦ Fire on the Rooftop ✦

Adélaïde and Oliver returned to their homes after agreeing to meet Archer on the Glubs' roof at eight o'clock.

"Slow down," said Mrs. Glub. "You'll go blind if you keep eating like that."

"He's hungry," said Mr. Glub. "I used to eat like that at his age."

"Used to?" said Mrs. Glub with a smile.

"I'm hungry," laughed Mr. Glub. "He'll eat like this at my age."

"We're all sleeping at Oliver's tonight," Adélaïde told her father. "Just in case you need me."

"Sounds like a good time," Mr. Belmont replied. "By the way, did you ever happen across that polar bear?"

"I did," said Adélaïde. "It's actually quite nice."

Archer ate quietly. His father, as usual, was working late in the study and his mother was fussing over a stain on a linen napkin that wouldn't come out no matter how she tried.

"It's Mrs. Murkley's lipstick," she said. "And it *still* won't come out."

When he finished, he set to work, timing his movements with his mother's. First he lugged the metal bowl from the cellar to the roof, which was more difficult than he thought it would be. He finally got it up the ladder, though, and returned to the roof shortly with two sleeping bags and pillows. His final trip was into the sitting room to collect wood from the fireplace. Once his arms were full, he hurried up the stairs and straight into Mr. Helmsley, who had just stepped from his study.

"What's all that for?" he asked with an odd twinkle in his eye. "Hope you're not planning to set the roof on fire."

Archer dropped the wood and nearly fell backward down the stairs. "I'm—why did you say that?"

Mr. Helmsley grinned. "No reason," he replied. "Just be careful."

Archer stood quietly, watching his father saunter down the stairs. He slowly gathered the logs and climbed to the roof. Oliver and Adélaïde were waiting for him. Oliver looked annoyed. Adélaïde was laughing.

"What's going on?" Archer asked.

Oliver groaned and took a seat on his sleeping bag.

"My father told her the Rosewood Zoo story," he said. "When I was four and that monkey pulled my head through the bars."

"Did that really happen?" said Archer, trying not to laugh.

"Yes, they had to cut the bars to get me out," said Oliver. "That place is horrible. It's a wonder they're still in business with the way they run things."

"'Now you mustn't get too close to the bars, *Ollie*,'" Adélaïde giggled, imitating Mrs. Glub.

Oliver went pink.

"Please don't call me that," he said. "I hate it when they call me that."

Archer smiled and dropped his pile of wood on top of Oliver's.

The sun was gone and the stars were out, and they had to use flashlights to see what they were doing. Both Archer and Oliver had made fires in their fireplaces before, but making a fire on the rooftop in the wind proved a bit more challenging. They argued over the specifics, and after a number of failed attempts, Archer managed to get a small fire sparkling in the metal bowl. Adélaide hovered over them with a bucket of water while Oliver tore pieces of *The Doldrums Press* to help it along.

"Listen to this," he said.

THE DOLDRUMS PRESS

GIRL VANISHES DOWN WISHING WELL

"That's awful," said Adélaïde.

Oliver agreed. He tore the story out and tossed it into the flames.

The fire was now doing quite well, but Archer wouldn't stop fiddling and poking at it.

"You have to let it breathe," said Oliver. "Take that stick off the top and put it over there."

"I think it's burning fine," said Adélaïde.

Archer finally agreed and left well enough alone. He moved the pile of wood next to his sleeping bag and tossed new logs on the fire whenever it slowed. All things considered, the fire burned nicely in that metal bowl and they pulled their sleeping bags in tight around it, watching as the flames flickered and the wood popped.

"How long did you say the voyage would be?" Oliver asked.

"About three weeks," said Archer.

"And how long are we going to be there?" Adélaïde asked.

"I'm not sure," said Archer. "But it can't be more than a month or two."

"That's a long time," said Oliver.

"Especially with one change of clothes," said Adélaïde.

"Well, it is the bottom of the world," said Archer.

"What keeps the blood from rushing to our heads?" Oliver asked.

"Gravity," said Archer. "There is no real top or bottom to the world. Someone drew it that way and everyone agreed to keep doing so."

"Either way," said Oliver. "It's a long trip. I've never traveled anywhere for that long."

"What do you think the captain will do when he finds out we've snuck aboard?" Adélaïde asked.

"We'll have to hide out for a few days," said Archer. "At least until we're far enough away that they won't turn back. Then we'll make ourselves known and I'll explain."

"We'll need to pack food for that," said Adélaïde.

Oliver, who'd been looking a little uncertain, brightened after hearing that and dug into his sleeping bag. He pulled out a bag of marshmallows and three sticks and they toasted them in silence. Adélaïde poked the gooey end of her stick into the embers and twisted it slowly.

"What if your grandparents are frozen to the iceberg?" she asked.

Archer leaned back on his sleeping bag. He knew it was a possibility, but he didn't like to think about it.

"I'll chip them free and bring them home," he said. "They deserve a proper burial."

Adélaïde nodded, but continued twisting her stick in the embers.

"I think you should leave them," she said. "You were right when you said their trunks didn't belong in a hole in the wall. They've spent their entire lives traveling the world and they could continue doing so on their iceberg. I think they'd like that better than being stuck in the ground."

Archer straightened and, though he wasn't hungry, poked another marshmallow onto his stick.

"You're right," he said, putting his marshmallows into the flames.

The trio continued talking long into the night until eventually, they all fell asleep.

✦

In the morning, all three of them woke a little chilled and a little damp, but only Archer woke up with a pigeon nesting on his face.

"Don't move," whispered Oliver, inching toward him with a stick.

Archer shooed the creature away—more afraid of Oliver's stick than a pigeon. There were feathers in his hair and feathers on the pillow. He brushed them away while trying to figure out why the bird chose him. Oliver and Adélaïde were too busy laughing to offer any good suggestions.

"Didn't you feel it?" Adélaïde asked.

"He's a sound sleeper," said Oliver.

After shaking away their morning stupor and the last of the feathers, Oliver went downstairs to get a kettle and a pot for oatmeal. Archer also went downstairs to make an appearance so his mother wouldn't come looking for him. But in the kitchen, he kept his distance, afraid his mother would smell the smoke.

Adélaïde stayed on the roof staring at her house across the gardens. She didn't think about ballet anymore and was surprised this didn't bother her as much as she thought it would. But she was growing more uncomfortable with lying to Archer and Oliver. Only her father knew the truth—her father and Miss Whitewood. It had slipped out one afternoon.

"It was a bakery truck," she said. "A bakery truck and a lamppost."

"Did you really think I believed the crocodile story?" Miss Whitewood asked.

Adélaïde didn't. "That's why I wanted to say it," she replied. "But everyone else believes it and I don't want to lie anymore."

"Do you think everyone believes it?"

Adélaïde didn't know who believed it and who didn't. But Archer and Oliver did and they were the ones she wanted to tell, but couldn't. Not now at least.

When Archer and Oliver returned to the roof, they made a second fire and boiled the tea and oatmeal. It didn't taste as good as when they made it in the house but they ate it all the same.

"I feel good after sleeping on a hard surface," said Oliver.

Archer agreed. Adélaïde said she felt stiff. She stood up to stretch, and both Archer and Oliver were impressed at how well she did—standing on the tip of her wooden leg and sticking the other straight out. But then she lost her balance and fell back onto her sleeping bag.

"Where did you learn how to do that?" Archer asked.

"You almost looked like a ballerina," said Oliver.

"Girls can stretch better than boys," she said, searching her oatmeal for a raisin while Oliver watched her from the corner of his eye.

None of them wanted to leave, so they stayed together and talked and laughed and let the morning pass without a word about Antarctica or what was coming tomorrow. But as morning turned into early afternoon, and because tomorrow was the day of days, they eventually cleaned up and went their separate ways.

• Quiet •

Archer spent the rest of the day in his room. He took a bath to wash away the smoke, but afterward decided not to return downstairs. He stretched out on his bed wondering what tomorrow would bring. He wasn't certain. But he was certain that if something went wrong, if they didn't make it onto that ship, he would be in more trouble than he'd ever been in before. He was disobeying his parents, he had forged their signatures, he was running away from Willow Street, and he was boarding a ship to Antarctica. It was a lot. But it was worth it. He only wished they were more ready.

A paper airplane floated in through the window and

landed next to him. Archer, now used to this form of communication, read the note without sitting up.

Archer,
My father smelled me and asked if the Glubs' chimney was broken or if that's what their house always smells like. I've packed the food. We'll need a good breakfast. I don't know what will happen tomorrow, but I want to thank you for asking me to help. And I know you don't think we're ready, but we're more ready than you think we are.
Adélaïde

Archer left his bed and sat down at his desk to write a letter back.

Adélaïde,
I was afraid my parents would smell the smoke too, but I don't think I'll go back downstairs. I sometimes think they can read my thoughts. I agree. We'll be okay tomorrow, but if we don't make it, there's a good chance I'll be locked away in a hole like the trunks or worse—probably worse. So I want to thank you now just in case.
Archer

Oliver stopped by Archer's room later that evening and they both climbed to the rooftop.

"I'm going to miss this place," Oliver said.

"I'm glad you're coming," said Archer. "Are you ready?"

"I'm not," Oliver replied. "Though I'll never be ready so it's fine. But I hope you are."

"I'm ready," said Archer.

There was nothing else they could do except sit and wait, and that's never an easy thing. When you're busy with preparations, you don't have time to second-guess yourself. But when you're sitting quietly with the task still ahead of you, your mind begins to warn you of all the things that can go wrong. They were all correct to think they were underprepared. It was obvious they were. But Oliver and Adélaïde were right. They were more prepared than they thought they were, and they would never be fully prepared because that's impossible. Still, when night fell on crooked, narrow Willow Street, Archer, Oliver, and Adélaïde all struggled to fall asleep. They had all slept much better when they were together around the fire.

CHAPTER

SIXTEEN

• A Southern Gale •

The wind blew leaves from the trees and howled across the roofs as the sun rose over Willow Street. It was the morning of the escape. Archer, Oliver, and Adélaïde went about their separate businesses. Adélaïde left her bag by the door and stepped into the kitchen. She scooped a heap of dog food from a sack. Her father was rummaging through the cabinets.

"Have you seen my espresso cups and spoons, Adié?" he asked.

"I haven't," she replied, and poured the food into a bowl.

A dirty Fritz galloped in through the garden doors and plopped his face into that bowl. Adélaïde stared at her father, unsure what to say, but knowing she couldn't leave without saying anything.

"I'll be going away for a while," she said as her father

bent down to check beneath the sink. "But it shouldn't be too long."

"That's nice," said Mr. Belmont, straightening himself and pressing his hands to his back. "Where could they have gone?" he mumbled.

Across the gardens, Oliver was having a difficult time finishing his breakfast. He'd been up late the night before trying to figure out everything that could go wrong, but the list went on and on and his hand cramped and he fell asleep on his desk.

"You've barely eaten a thing," said Mrs. Glub.

"Less to lose later," said Oliver.

Mr. Glub poured himself a large cup of coffee and sat down. "Are you planning on losing it?" he asked.

"I don't know what I'm planning on," said Oliver.

Next door, Archer was having a much easier time finishing his breakfast. You'd never know it by looking at him, but he was bursting with excitement. He was finally about to do something great. Mr. Helmsley had left for work and his mother was seated across from him. He finished his breakfast, told her he'd be upstairs reading (while the rest of his class was at the museum), and grabbed the badger on his way up the stairs.

"Where are you taking me?" asked the badger.

"I need you to be me," said Archer.

"I'd rather eat hot coals than be you," said the ostrich when Archer came back for the fox.

Archer nodded. "We finally agree on something," he replied.

Archer shut his bedroom door. Oliver was on the balcony. He stepped into the room. Archer pulled aside his bedsheets and placed the badger and the fox head to toe.

"What do you think your mother will do when she finds out?" Oliver asked.

"I don't know," he replied. "But we have to get to Rosewood Port before she does. We'll have time."

Archer scribbled two notes. One he gave to Oliver, who turned it into an airplane and sent it to Adélaïde. The other was a letter of explanation to his parents. He placed that letter in the badger's paw before pulling the covers over its head.

Archer and Oliver climbed the ladder to the roof, took one final look into the gardens, and ducked into Oliver's house. Archer waited just inside the front door for Oliver's signal before slipping out of the house.

The wind whirled down the sidewalk. Adélaïde's hair, which usually fell neatly across her forehead, was swirling with it, every which way at once. Oliver thought she looked like a madwoman, but he and Archer were glad to see her.

The crocodile girl gave them confidence and a chocolate croissant each. They finished them before arriving at the Button Factory. Students were assembled on the front steps. Mrs. Murkley towered over them, keeping a watchful eye.

School trips are supposed to be exciting affairs, but the students' expressions would make you think otherwise.

"I don't think we're going to the museum," said Charlie H. Brimble. "She's probably taking us to Rosewood Cliffs to hurl us into the ocean."

"Let's pretend to be sick," said Molly S. Mellings.

"I don't have to pretend," said Alice P. Suggins.

✦ According to Plan ✦

Archer, Oliver, and Adélaïde joined the miserable group and stood as far from Mrs. Murkley as they could. Archer opened his notebook to review the plan one last time.

The first step was to sneak away during their tour of the museum. Archer would go first, followed by Adélaïde, and Oliver would pull up the rear. They would meet next to Tappenkuse with their masks in place and, once they were all together, make for the back exit and Rosewood Park. After winding their way through the unruly park, they would follow the canal to Rosewood Port, where they would wait for the guard to leave his booth. Then they would locate Dock E7, where hopefully the research vessel would still be loading cargo. They would climb atop a pallet and wait to be loaded onto the ship. Once aboard, they would find a place to hide until the ship was too far out to sea to turn back. Adélaïde had packed enough food to last them three days. After that, they would make themselves known. Archer would ask to speak to the ship's captain and would explain why they were there and what they came to do. And whether the captain liked it or not, they would be on their way to Antarctica. That was their plan.

Mrs. Murkley ordered the class into two lines and they followed her down the sidewalk, into Rosewood Park, and up the museum steps.

• The Great Hall •

The students pushed through the museum doors and stared with eyes wide at the brilliant great hall. It was massive, with all manner of beasts and insects and ornate murals. Everyone began whispering. Archer was quiet. Mrs. Murkley approached the counter to get their tickets.

"I'll need sixteen," she said, but was handed thirty-two.

"And what's this?" she huffed, eyeing the extras.

"We're currently in a partnership with the Rosewood

Zoo," chirped the woman behind the counter. "Each week they bring a different species of animal into our special exhibit space and discuss the creatures. You will then be able to see displays about the animal's evolution and historical significance elsewhere in the museum. Everyone will love it. All the classes have."

"Very well," said Mrs. Murkley, making it quite clear she wouldn't love it. "And what's this week's creature? Newts?"

"Tigers!"

Mrs. Murkley glanced over her shoulder at Archer, Adélaïde, and Oliver, who were all too busy staring around the great hall to notice.

"Tigers," she mumbled. "*Perfect.*"

With the tickets in hand, Mrs. Murkley barked and the students followed her down the corridor to the special exhibit space. Archer grabbed three maps from the counter and handed one to Oliver and one to Adélaïde.

"This is where Tappenkuse is," he said, circling the spot on both their maps with a pen. He looked at Mrs. Murkley. She didn't know where she was going. He nodded, pulled his bag tight, and gave his friends an uncertain smile.

"This is it," he said. "I'll see you on the other side."

Archer dashed into the Hall of Reptiles and put on his badger mask. Mrs. Murkley didn't see a thing.

The class turned a corner and continued down another corridor. Oliver was growing pale.

"Don't worry," said Adélaïde, placing a hand on his shoulder. "You'll be brilliant."

She hesitated a moment, then clomped down the Hall of Night Creatures while securing her lion mask.

Oliver continued on alone. And that's exactly how he felt.

⋅ A Special Exhibit ⋅

Archer hurried down a corridor and entered the Egyptian Wing to take his position next to Tappenkuse. He felt strange with everyone staring at him so he pushed the badger mask up on his head. While he waited for Adélaïde, he unzipped his bag and pulled out the jade elephant house. He was thinking about his grandparents when Adélaïde tapped his shoulder. He nearly screamed.

"Sorry," she said, lifting her lion mask. "It's a little difficult to see in these, isn't it?"

"I thought so too," he replied. "And everyone was staring at me."

They fell silent. Both of them were anxious to escape the museum and began looking around the room, hoping Oliver wouldn't be far behind.

⋅

The students arrived at the special exhibit space as expected. Oliver was still with them, which was unexpected. He'd been too afraid to leave and didn't know what to do. Mrs. Murkley began handing out the special exhibit tickets, but had two left over.

"All right," she growled. "Who doesn't have a ticket?"

No one said anything.

"Hold up your tickets!"

Everyone had a ticket. Mrs. Murkley scanned the group and spotted Oliver standing alone. He wasn't alone when they began. He was never alone.

"You!" she barked. "Where are your comrades?"

Oliver was panicking on the inside, but tried his best to look calm.

"Who, me?" he asked. "They're not with me. Please don't put me on your list."

Mrs. Murkley plowed toward him, looking as though she might hurl him into the Hall of Invertebrates. Oliver thought about running, but froze instead.

"I can see they're not *with* you," she snapped. "But they were *with* you when we started. And if you don't tell me where they are, you'll be *with* them on my list."

Oliver's inner turmoil overtook his outer calm, but he couldn't betray Archer and Adélaïde. He had to stick to the plan.

"They're in the bathroom," he said, wishing they'd thought up a better excuse. "If you give me their tickets, I can wait here and—"

"They're going to Antarctica!" Charlie Brimble shouted.

Mr. Murkley glared at him. Charlie shrank.

"At least—I think they are."

"That's impossible," said Oliver.

Mrs. Murkley grabbed Oliver by the shoulders and ushered him into the special exhibit room. Once everyone else was inside, she threw the tickets at the guard and said, "None of them are to leave." Then she stormed off in search of trouble.

• Gaudy Little Fellow •

Archer and Adélaïde were still next to Tappenkuse. Archer was growing worried.

"He should have been here by now," he said.

"I'm sure he's on his way," Adélaïde replied.

They stepped away from the sarcophagus and searched a corridor, hoping to see Oliver or a gazelle. They didn't. But they turned back just in time to see Mrs. Murkley march into the room.

"Something's happened!" said Archer.

"To Oliver?" said Adélaïde.

"We have to go."

Archer grabbed her hand. They ran from the Egyptian Wing and ducked into the Hall of Ungulates. In his rush, Archer didn't notice the jade elephant house fall from his bag. A janitor watched this happen. He picked it up, slipped it into his jumpsuit pocket, and was about to go after them when the museum director, who was making his rounds, quickly jumped in front of him.

"Are you stealing from the museum?" the director asked.

"I wasn't," said the janitor. "It's only—"

The director reached into the janitor's pocket and removed the jade figurine. *"I see."* He signaled for the two security guards and said, "Take him to pack his things."

The guards nodded. Each took one of his arms.

"But it doesn't belong to the museum!" said the janitor. "It's not—it's the—*Thai Ferry*!"

Archer and Adélaïde were hiding behind a mountain goat when Mrs. Murkley stormed into the hall. Her eyes were hopping everywhere, but she didn't see them behind the pedestal. She continued across the room but when she reached the end, she stopped.

"Why isn't she leaving?" whispered Adélaïde.

"I think she smells us," said Archer.

Two guards entered the hall carrying the janitor roughly

by the arms. They dragged him through a door marked "Museum Personnel Only."

"Quick!" whispered Archer.

They crept behind a moose and slipped through the door before it closed. The guards were going down a spiraling stairwell. Archer and Adélaïde went up. They went up and up and up and pushed through a small door at the very top of a museum tower. The wind blew the masks from their heads and carried them deep into Rosewood Park. They ran full circle around the spire. There was nowhere else to go.

"I don't think we should go back that way," said Archer, pointing to the door. "She might still be there." He squinted far across the roof to where a second tower rose. "Do you think we can get over there?"

Adélaïde wasn't sure but she nodded. So Archer carefully helped her over the wall and then lowered himself to the roof. For a moment, neither of them moved. They were standing on a moldy strip of slate only two feet wide. The roof slanted steeply down on both sides. A slip from here would send them plummeting four stories.

"This wasn't a good idea," said Archer.

"We just have to be careful," said Adélaïde.

They joined hands and, with great care, began inching their way through the wind across the roof.

• Helmsley & Durbish •

Mr. Helmsley was in his office. His secretary was seated across from him taking notes.

"Are those children on the museum rooftop?" his secretary asked, pointing over his head and out the window.

Mr. Helmsley spun around and peered out the window. He removed his glasses, cleaned them against his shirt, and squinted once more. Sure enough, two figures *were* making their way across the rooftop. One figure slipped. The other helped it up. Both continued on.

"They're going to get themselves killed!"

"That almost looks like—" Mr. Helmsley spun back around. He asked his secretary to leave and picked up the phone.

"Is something wrong?" Mrs. Helmsley asked.

"I'm not sure," said Mr. Helmsley. "I just wanted to know if Archer was at home."

"Yes," she replied. "He's reading in his room."

"Can you check?"

Mrs. Helmsley set the phone down and went to Archer's room. There was a lump in the bed. She approached the lump and placed her hand on what should have been Archer's shoulder. It wasn't.

"He's a badger!" she yelled into the phone.

"He's a *what*?" asked Mr. Helmsley.

• Glittering Specks •

Archer and Adélaïde reached the opposite spire and took shelter from the wind in an arched alcove. They could see out across Rosewood Park. The shaggy trees gave way to the warehouses of Barrow's Bay and the canal. Beyond that they could just make out Rosewood Port and a glittering silver streak that was the sea. That's where they wanted to be, glittering specks on the glittering sea. And that would be simple if only they could sprout wings and fly from the roof. But they couldn't. So they stood with their backs pressed tight against the tower, watching as leaves swirled in the wind.

"At least she won't look up here," said Adélaïde.

"Neither will Oliver," Archer replied.

• Gazelle! Gazelle! •

Four stories below, an anxious Oliver was sitting in the special exhibit space. The room was like a greenhouse. It extended beyond the museum and into Rosewood Park, which loomed just beyond the wrought iron and glass walls. Oliver's eyes were fixed out those windows, hoping Adélaïde and Archer weren't running through the park without him. The other students were staring at the center of the room where a large wooden platform held a cage with three tigers that were staring straight back at the students.

How tasty, thought one.

Except for that String Bean, thought the second. *He's too lean to have much flavor.*

He'd make a good toothpick, thought the third. *To pry the chunks of that graceful swanlike one from our teeth.*

A glass door opened at the far end of the exhibit space and a man with a dolly wheeled a container toward the cage. Two more men lifted the container while a fourth opened it. Inside were all sorts of meats. Everyone leaned forward—everyone except Oliver. Oliver bent down and dug into his bag. He decided to make a run for it. One of the zoo workers unlatched the cage. Oliver stood up and secured his gazelle mask.

• One Polar Bear Too Many •

Archer and Adélaïde climbed down the tower and popped into the museum, but before Archer had even taken two steps, two massive hands clamped around his shoulders and squeezed tight. It was Mrs. Murkley. He couldn't believe it.

"What do you think you're doing?" she demanded, eyes blazing.

"Let him go!" said Adélaide. "You're going to ruin everything!"

"Ruin *what* everything?"

"We have to go!" said Archer.

"Go where?" she barked.

"It's none of your business," said Adélaïde.

"I'm your teacher," growled Mrs. Murkley. "Everything is *my* business. And the only place you two are going is back to my office!"

Mrs. Murkley swung a hand at Adélaïde, but she spun a lopsided pirouette. She tripped over her wooden leg

and crashed into a pedestal hosting a massive polar bear. The bear wobbled back and forth. Mrs. Murkley moved in to grab Adélaïde.

"You can't know the *joy* I will take in stuffing the two of you into—"

"Look out!" someone shouted.

"It's going to fall!" yelled someone else.

The polar bear leaned forward. Mrs. Murkley leaned backward. She released Archer and threw up her hands. Archer jumped. Mrs. Murkley didn't. But she let out a shriek when the polar bear began its journey south, straight into her outstretched arms. It was a formidable match, but Mrs. Murkley was defeated—smashed to the floor beneath the massive polar bear.

Archer lifted Adélaïde up off the ground. A crowd swooped in on the scene. Everyone stared at the tangled mass of Murkley and polar bear.

"I think she's dead."

"I've never seen a dead person before."

"It can't look much different."

"Should we roll it off her?"

The crowd agreed that would be most sensible, so a handful of strangers rolled the creature off the woman. Mrs. Murkley had gone completely white in the face. The crowd waited in silence. Then, very slowly, two tiny slits opened to her eyes.

"She's alive!"

"A solid woman, that is!"

"They don't make 'em like that anymore!"

Mrs. Murkley lifted her head and scanned the surrounding horde, passing from one person to the next till she found the two she was searching for. Archer and Adélaïde remained silent. Mrs. Murkley let out a groan and mumbled, "Criminals—that's what you are." Only it didn't sound like that at all. The crowd leaned forward.

"What did she say?"

"I think she said, 'Criminal rats cut blue jars.'"

"What does that mean?"

"It means she's been knocked senseless—her screws are loose."

"They do still make 'em like that."

Mrs. Murkley lowered her head to the ground. The polar bear was next to her, but no one seemed concerned about it.

"What are you waiting for?" the bear whispered to Archer. "Run!"

Archer nodded. He took one last look at Mrs. Murkley before pulling Adélaïde through the crowd.

"We have to go now or we're never going to make it," he whispered. "This is becoming a nightmare."

They ran back to the gaudy little fellow, hoping Oliver would be waiting for them.

• These Sorts of Things Don't Happen •

Oliver still wasn't there. Archer and Adélaïde stayed together while searching the Egyptian Wing, but there was no sign of him anywhere so they wandered into the corridor.

"I don't understand," said Archer. "He knew the plan."

"There he is!" said Adélaïde.

Archer spun around. Oliver was barreling down the corridor straight toward them. But his eyes were shut and no sooner had Adélaïde spotted him than he smashed straight into her. Adélaïde screeched across the floor. Archer, who didn't let go of her hand, went with her.

"Sorry!" said Oliver, opening his eyes to see what he hit this time.

"That's all right," said a shaken Adélaïde. "Do you always run with your eyes closed?"

"Only when he's late," said Archer.

Oliver helped them both up off the ground, but they were

more concerned about him. Oliver was breathing heavily, his mask was gone, and panic, unlike any they'd seen, was flickering in his eyes.

"Are you okay?" asked Archer.

Oliver spoke between breaths. "Chaos everywhere—threw mask—distraction!"

"The masks were terrible, weren't they?" said Adélaïde, trying to help him along.

"At least we're together," said Archer. "Now let's get out of here."

"Wait," said Adélaïde. "What happened to your arm?"

Oliver's arm was bleeding, but he wasn't yet able to explain that when he tore off his mask and threw it, he ran straight into a pedestal holding a glass box with a jeweled egg inside. The egg cracked in two and glass shattered everywhere.

"I'm fine," he managed. "It's fine."

Adélaïde wasn't convinced. There was a lot of blood. She pulled her only extra shirt from her bag to wrap around Oliver's arm, but froze when shouts and cries echoed down the corridor. Oliver winced and glanced over his shoulder. Adélaïde and Archer looked over his shoulder as well. Down that corridor, but not a long way off, a pack of tigers were slipping and sliding across the marble floor straight toward them.

"You didn't!" said Archer, not believing what he was seeing.

"I did," sighed Oliver.

"But how?!" said Adélaïde.

There certainly were many questions to answer, but now was not the time for that. They should have been running or hiding like everyone else aware of the situation unfolding. But they were in shock and not a single logical thought passed though their collective brains. They simply stood there, staring at the approaching tigers with hearts beating like hummingbird wings. Out of nowhere and as if by instinct, Oliver shouted "*Survival kit!*" It didn't make sense, but that's what happened. He threw down his bag. He knew the instructions. He yanked the string. They all stood back.

An inflatable life raft was not what Oliver was hoping for. It wasn't what Archer or Adélaïde were hoping for either. But that's what they got. And while most would agree that a life raft would be of little use in this situation, the raft did do something remarkable. The sudden flash of yellow, the whooshing of air, and the thunderous thump when it hit the floor startled the approaching tigers and they slid to a halt. You could never know for certain, but it's likely the tigers thought the raft was a creature much larger than themselves. And while this was a terrific bit of luck, a six-foot piece of inflatable plastic was not the ideal barrier.

Archer, Adélaïde, and Oliver stood motionless. Not one dared to blink. But their minds slowly began to turn once more and Archer and Oliver were thinking the same thing, *We have the crocodile girl!*

Careful not to take his eyes off the tiger, Archer whispered to Adélaïde, "What should we do?"

Adélaïde didn't respond.

"What did you do with the crocodiles?" said Oliver.

Adélaïde didn't respond.

She's forming a plan? they hoped.

"I was lying about the crocodiles," she whispered. "I've never even seen a crocodile."

"Of course you have," said Oliver.

"One ate your leg," said Archer.

"I was hit by a lamppost."

"A lamppost?" repeated Oliver.

"I was a ballerina."

"A ballerina?" said Archer.

Archer and Oliver fell silent once more. This would not do. They needed Adélaïde to be who she wasn't. They needed Adélaïde the great adventurer. They had Adélaïde the ballerina. And there's a big difference between surviving a crocodile and surviving a lamppost. A tiger slowly approached the raft. It was only a matter of time before it realized it was a lump of plastic and nothing more. The prevailing sentiment among Archer, Oliver, and Adélaïde was one of hopelessness. Absolute hopelessness.

The recently fired janitor finished packing his belongings and glanced over his shoulder at the guards who were discussing something of no importance. The janitor quietly slipped down the hall and into an office where the intercom system was located. After locking the door, he set a radio next to the microphone. He wasn't going anywhere without giving the museum director a piece of his mind.

• Bon Voyage •

All at once, music filled the museum. It echoed up the stairwells, poured down the corridors, and seeped out of opened windows and into Rosewood Park. Archer looked up. Adélaïde looked up. Oliver looked up. The tigers looked up. In fact, at that very moment, everyone in the museum was looking up, wondering what was going on.

Archer looked back at the tigers. He wasn't sure what to do, but thought the worst thing they could do was let the tigers make the first move.

"Slowly turn around," he whispered. "We have to make a run for it."

That was not well received.

"Not with this leg," said Adélaïde.

"You have to," he replied.

"What difference does it make," said Oliver. "If I'm not eaten today, I'm sure I'll be eaten tomorrow."

"I'd prefer tomorrow," said Archer.

Adélaïde agreed. It took him a moment, but Oliver also agreed. Then slowly, ever so slowly, they turned around. An odd sensation came over each of them—a sensation known only to those who've turned their backs on tigers. For a moment, no one said anything, not a word. They waited, certain that at any moment, claws would tear into their backs. But there was a flicker in Archer's eyes. And while only a fool would smile in such a situation, it seemed like that's what he wanted to do.

"Keep your eyes open," he said, studying the corridor ahead of them and the rooms shooting off either side. "But don't look back."

Archer and Oliver each took one of Adélaïde's hands.

"And don't go anywhere with carpet," Archer whispered. "They'll have more traction on carpet."

"Count to three?" said Adélaïde.

All three nodded. They gripped tightly.

Archer took a deep breath. "One," he said.

"*Deux,*" said Adélaïde.

"—THREE!"

✦ Wing of African Mammals ✦

They shot down the corridor like a champagne cork and were gone in a flash, bolting into the Wing of African Mammals. They barreled down the center aisle, passing dioramas on either side.

"Faster!" said Oliver. "I don't want to be in a diorama!"

They sprang through a doorway and hurled themselves down a flight of stairs, in what a woman standing nearby would later tell reporters appeared to be a single leap.

"This way!" said Archer. He pulled the others right and they flew into the Wing of Tropical Birds.

✦ Wing of Tropical Birds ✦

Two guards jumped from their chairs and raised their hands.

"Stop!" demanded one. The other blew his whistle.

But they didn't stop. They held their course, gripping one another's hands tighter still as they blasted past the guards.

"This uniform means nothing," said one of the guards.

The other continued blowing his whistle.

"They're gone!"

The whistler pointed at the tigers. Both guards abandoned their posts.

Archer, Oliver, and Adélaïde wove their way down a crowded narrow corridor, crashing into people left and right. Archer was shouting "*Tigers!*" but no one listened, choosing instead to glare disapprovingly at such rudeness. Their expressions changed, however, when someone spotted the tigers.

"*Insensé!*" said Adélaïde.

The crowd was everywhere at once, running and squawking like spooked chickens. "That way!" shouted Archer. He leaned right and spun the others back into the Egyptian Wing.

• Egyptian Wing •

A tour group was standing before Tappenkuse, blinding the gaudy little fellow with the flashes from their cameras. Archer, Oliver, and Adélaïde plowed their way through.

"Tigers!" said Archer.

"No," said a foolish man. "It's pronounced Tap-in-koos."

The man quickly dropped his camera and ran with everyone else when he realized what was happening. The trio ducked into an ancient ruin and shot out the other side. They dashed from the Egyptian wing and up a spiraling stair. At the top, Archer planted his feet, whipping Adélaïde and Oliver to the right and pouring them into the Wing of Ocean Life.

• Doldrums Press •

Mr. Glub was sitting at his desk, writing an article for the newspaper. Without notice, two journalists burst in.

"Tigers!" said one.

"Museum!" said the other.

Mr. Glub smiled and leaned back in his chair.

"Slow down," he said. "Now, what's this all about?"

When they finally got the story out, Mr. Glub jumped to his feet, grabbed his coat, and ran from the office with a reporter on either side.

• Wing of Ocean Life •

"How many wings does this place have?" said Oliver as they dashed beneath a massive octopus.

The music was still blaring from the intercoms, but then they heard an announcement, too:

"Please make your way to the nearest exit.
We ask everyone to calmly make their way to the nearest exit.
Please see a guard for help if needed."

Everyone was already moving to the exits, but there was nothing calm about it. Everywhere was panic. Some people were screaming, others were shouting, but everyone was running. Parents grabbed children. Others gave up and crouched in corners.

"Which way is the exit?" Oliver yelled, bouncing off a giant squid.

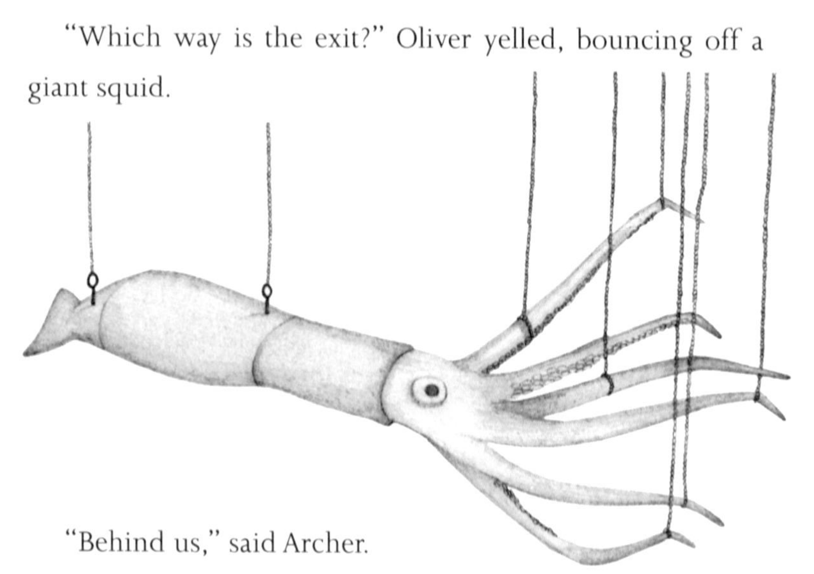

"Behind us," said Archer.

He broke his own rule and glanced over his shoulder. The tigers were slipping all over the place, but they were still very much after them. He didn't understand. Why were they the only ones being chased?

"We can't go back," he said as they spilled into a hall and down a flight of stairs. Oliver lost a shoe. It clopped a tiger on the head.

"That way!" said Archer.

They flew into the butterfly pavilion.

✦ Butterfly Pavilion ✦

They were growing tired as they dashed past row after row of neatly aligned butterfly boxes. Alarms were flashing and gates were slamming all around.

"They're going to lock us in!" said Adélaïde.

"With the tigers!" said Oliver.

"Not yet!" said Archer.

✦ Belmont Coffee & Café ✦

Mr. Belmont was too busy running his espresso machine to notice the hordes of people fleeing Rosewood Park. The flowery woman wasn't. She spun around on her barstool and almost began clapping.

"Oh! Look!" she cried. "It's a parade! I do so very much love a parade! But it's a *strange* parade—yes, a very strange one indeed."

Mr. Belmont dashed outside. This was no parade. He looked up at the museum towers. Someone yelled "*Tiger!*"

Mr. Belmont took off. The flowery woman slipped behind the bar to make herself a triple.

• The Not-So-Great Hall •

They were running much slower when they burst back into the great hall. It had emptied, and security gates blocked the exits.

"We're trapped!" said Adélaïde.

"With the tigers!" said Oliver.

"To the kiosk!" said Archer.

A round kiosk stood at the center of the hall. They ran in a tight circle around it. The tigers followed but slid all over the place. There was nowhere else to go. A row of telephone booths stood to their right. Archer planted his feet and whipped the others toward the booths.

"Get inside and shut the doors," he yelled.

They held tightly to one another till the last possible second, then all three let go, leaped into the booths, and slammed the doors. The tigers crashed against the booths. Phones flew off the hooks. Oliver had his eyes shut. Adélaïde was on the seat with her wooden leg pressed tightly against her door, trying to keep it shut. Archer dodged a swinging phone but struck his head hard against the wall. Everything went black.

✦ The Museum Director ✦

"Archer," said Adélaïde.

"Archer?" said Oliver.

"Is he okay?"

"I don't know."

Archer opened his eyes. He was sitting crumpled in a cold sweat, but he didn't know where he was. Oliver and Adélaïde were studying him.

"Did we make it to the ship?" he asked.

"No," said Adélaïde.

"Not even close," said Oliver.

"Out of the way!" ordered a security guard, pushing Adélaïde and Oliver to the side. He noticed Oliver's arm and pointed to a nurse. "Have her take a look at that."

Adélaïde followed Oliver to the nurse. Archer was still trying to make sense of everything as the guard reached out his hand.

Two guards escorted Archer, Oliver, and Adélaïde through a door and down a back hallway. They had been summoned to the director's office. Archer was still fuzzy, but nearly back to his senses.

"What happened after we jumped in the booths?" he asked.

"I thought it was over," said Oliver. "Until zoo personnel burst in with tranquilizers."

"We stayed inside the booths," said Adélaïde. "But they saw us."

"I thought they were going to tranquilize us when they did," Oliver said.

Adélaïde nodded. "We're in a great deal of trouble."

At the top of a staircase, one of their guards knocked on a door and they entered a large, dusty office with a giant window that overlooked the great hall. A man who could only be the director of the museum was standing next to his desk, speaking with two more guards. He paused when they entered. Archer didn't like the way he stared at them. It made him feel like a criminal. The director turned back to the guards. "Just bring it to me," he said, and sent them out while motioning the trio to come forward.

"Take a seat," he instructed, pointing to a bench beside his desk.

Archer, Oliver, and Adélaïde did so and the director gave them a chance to speak.

"It just sort of happened," said Oliver.

"It wasn't our fault," said Archer. "But we did great."

Adélaïde chose not to say anything.

"No one was eaten," agreed the director, sitting back

down. "But there's a lot of middle ground between not getting eaten and something being great."

That wasn't what Archer meant, but before he could clarify, a guard reentered the office and handed the director a report. The director secured his glasses and mumbled quietly as he read.

"Which of you is Oliver Glub?" he asked.

Oliver slowly raised his hand.

"And what exactly were you thinking, bringing a gazelle mask into a room filled with tigers?"

Oliver turned to Archer and Adélaïde for support. He was never good when adults questioned him.

"The mask didn't matter," Adélaïde said. "What matters is how the tigers were able to escape. Weren't they chained down?"

The director pinched his lips and grunted. "I'm looking into it," he replied. "We've already cancelled the partnership." He returned to the report and a few lines later, pointed a finger at Archer and Adélaïde. "And I assume, then, that you two were the ones on the museum rooftop?"

"You were on the roof?!" said Oliver.

"We didn't know where we were going," said Archer.

"Not until we got there," said Adélaïde.

"You went through a 'Museum Personnel Only' door,"

said the director. "I expect you knew that much."

Archer and Adélaïde were silent. They did know that much.

"And the *life raft*!" shouted the director. "How did you get that thing inside the museum?!"

Oliver was surprised about that too. "It wasn't heavy," he said. "But I also didn't know it was a raft until I pulled the string. To be honest, I wasn't sure what it was."

"But why did you have it in the museum?" the director demanded. "No one needs a life raft in a museum!"

"*We* did," said Adélaïde.

"We would be dead without it," said Archer.

The director grunted again. "Do you have any idea the amount of damage you've inflicted on my museum?" he asked. "A two-thousand-year-old jeweled egg was cracked, there is glass all over the place, the tigers smashed more things than could be listed on this report, and hundreds were nearly killed!"

"We were just trying to get out of the way," said Adélaïde. "It wasn't our fault the tigers broke free."

"And they were only chasing us," said Archer. "I don't know why."

The director pointed at Oliver's now-bandaged arm. "Blood and gazelles," he said. "It's a dangerous combination. And by the way, which of you is a *Helmsley*?"

"I am," said Archer. "I'm Archer Helmsley."

The director stared at him over the top of his glasses. "Of course you are," he said, shaking his head. "Don't remember me, do you?"

Archer had never met this man before and said just that.

"I've been to Helmsley House," he replied. "I was there the night you placed the porcupine on that man's chair."

Archer went red. He'd forgotten about the Glob of Seal. Adélaïde and Oliver looked at each other, trying not to smile. Archer noticed his jade elephant house sitting on the desk.

"I think that's mine," he said, pointing to it.

"What do you mean it's *yours*?"

"It was from my grandparents," Archer explained. "I must have dropped it."

The director blinked at him, then picked up the phone with a sigh. ". . . There's been a misunderstanding. . . . I know what *I* said. . . . Just get him back here, please." He tossed the jade elephant house at Archer and placed the report into his breast pocket. "The rest of your class has returned to school," he said. "Your teacher, Mrs.—Mrs.—"

"Murkley," said Adélaïde.

"Yes, well, the poor woman was discovered on the floor next to a polar bear. We assume she ran into it during the chaos."

"Another polar bear?" mumbled Oliver.

Archer and Adélaïde were silent.

"We think it fell on her. Nearly killed her." He looked at his watch and opened the door. "Now follow me. Your parents are waiting for you." He flashed Archer an unpleasant smile. "And I'm glad it's not me they're waiting for."

They followed the director back to the great hall and down the museum steps. People were standing everywhere. No one was happy. They followed him to the edge of Rosewood Park and to the street where Mrs. Murkley was being loaded into the back of an ambulance.

"Is she all right?" asked Archer.

"There's always hope," said the director. "But no one can understand a word she's saying."

The director opened a taxicab door and told them to get in.

"We live close," said Archer. "We can walk."

"That's what your mother was afraid of," the director said, ushering them into the backseat. "Get in. All of you. Mind your fingers!" He slammed the door and instructed the driver to take them to 375 Willow Street and to make sure they were all inside the house before leaving.

The taxi drove off.

CHAPTER

SEVENTEEN

✦ Ballerina's Spin ✦

"Well, that couldn't have gone worse," said Oliver. "We nearly died. You nearly died twice. We destroyed the museum. And seriously damaged Mrs. Murkley."

Despite all of this, there was a general air of gladness to be alive in the back of that taxicab. But Archer knew his current status as a member of the living was only temporary. And while he wasn't certain what awaited him at home, he was certain it was either a hole in the wall or Raven Wood.

Adélaïde scratched the dried blood on Oliver's blazer.

"Does it hurt?" she asked.

"Not really," he replied.

"What exactly happened in the tiger room?"

Oliver ran his finger across the window. "I honestly don't remember," he said. "It was difficult to see through those eyeholes. I heard—" He stopped and turned to Adélaïde. "Never mind that! What about the crocodile? You've been lying to us for a long time! I had a feeling you were."

"I guess your mother wasn't eaten either, was she?" asked Archer.

"No," said Adélaïde. "She's still very much alive."

"You were a ballerina?" asked Oliver.

Adélaïde nodded.

"What happened with the lamppost?" asked Archer.

She didn't want to talk about it, but she did. And while it would be a lie to say this didn't make her sad, she didn't feel as sad as she thought she would.

"Were you any good?" Oliver asked.

"I was pretty good," she replied.

The taxi turned down Willow Street. Archer had a tremendous knot in his stomach. After everything and all their planning, he couldn't even make it out of a museum. He slumped back into his seat, thinking about the iceberg.

"I hope their best is better than mine," he said.

"It's my fault," said Oliver.

"I'm the one who lied to you both," said Adélaïde.

"Maybe not the tigers," said Archer. "But the rest was my fault."

"We did this together," said Adélaïde.

After that, no one said anything.

• 375 Willow Street •

What followed when they arrived at Helmsley House was now only a blurry memory. They were slow crawling out of the backseat and slower still walking up the front steps. They paused at the doorknob and after a communal nod, pushed open the door. Inside, there were lots of adults shouting lots of things and while it was a lot to take in, compared with the tigers, they didn't think it was so bad.

"Does this sort of thing happen often here?" asked Mr. Belmont.

"Not that I know of," chuckled Mr. Glub. "I don't think many people can say they outran a pack of tigers."

"I never did," said Mr. Helmsley.

"Listen to them!" shrieked Mrs. Helmsley. "They've all got one foot off the merry-go-round!"

"It's good to stretch the foot from time to time," said Mr. Glub.

"Tea," said Mrs. Glub. "I think we all need tea—lots of tea."

"Or espresso," said Mr. Belmont.

"You could have died!" cried Mrs. Helmsley.

"But we didn't," said Archer.

"It just happened," said Oliver.

"We did good," said Adélaïde.

• A Scarlet Trunk •

Two weeks had passed since that nightmare of nightmares, and it now seemed like an impossible dream. Archer went to the cellar, emptied a scarlet trunk, and carried it back to his room to pack his things. The train for Raven Wood left in three days.

Mr. Helmsley stepped into the room just as he was finishing. He had dark circles under his eyes. The phones at Helmsley & Durbish had been ringing nonstop since the tiger incident and most days a line of people waiting to file lawsuits against the Rosewood Zoo wrapped around the office. The head of the zoo had been fired and they were currently undergoing major changes.

Mr. Helmsley sat down on the bed and Archer decided to tell his father everything he had discovered. There was no reason for him to keep it a secret anymore.

"I know Grandma and Grandpa were living in Barrow's Bay," he said. "And I know Mom sent them away after I was born because she didn't want them around me."

His father didn't bother asking how he'd discovered any

of this. But there were a few corrections to make.

"They were living in Barrow's Bay," he replied. "But your mother didn't send them anywhere. She couldn't. We didn't live in this house before you were born."

Archer glanced over the lid of his trunk. "Why do we live here now?" he asked.

"Your grandparents wanted us to move in after you were born. They wanted you to grow up in this house. Your grandfather had big ideas for you." Mr Helmsley paused. "Your grandparents are very good people, but they're part of a strange world. A world filed with many *peculiar* people—people that make your grandparents seem commonplace."

"The Society, you mean?"

Mr. Helmsley rubbed his chin and raised an eyebrow.

"The Society," he repeated. "I trust you haven't been there?"

"No," said Archer.

"Yes, well, the Society is a big part of it. But also your mother and I agreed that we wanted to be the ones to raise you. Not your grandparents. So we said no."

"But we did move in," said Archer.

"Yes, your grandfather is a very persuasive man," Mr. Helmsley replied, and folded his arms. "After we declined the first offer, he quickly made a second."

"What was it?" Archer asked.

"He promised they would stay away until your twelfth birthday if we would take the house. It took him some time to persuade your mother, but she eventually agreed and in we moved. Of course, no one had any idea they were going to wander onto an iceberg before your twelfth birthday." Mr. Helmsley smiled. "But that's very much your grandparents. And while they might be a little reckless, they knew *exactly* what they were doing getting you into Helmsley House. They didn't have to be here. Their magic is in these walls. They knew the house would raise you. Your mother realized this as well when she overheard you speaking to the animals. That's why she wanted you at all those dinner parties. She wanted you to start speaking to humans. Only you were never very good at that, were you?"

Archer grinned, though he tried not to. Mr. Helmsley's eyes suddenly twinkled. "But you did meet your grandfather. And you know you did."

"At the dinner party," said Archer, nodding. "How do you know about that?"

"He wanted to get a good look at you. I snuck him inside for a quick visit."

Archer sat atop his trunk and stared glumly at his father.

"I still don't understand why we couldn't have shared the house with them," he said.

"Right or wrong, that's what we decided. Like I said, it was our job to raise you, not theirs. And had we shared the house, many of their strange associates would have been coming and going. Your mother and I both agreed you shouldn't grow up around all of that."

"But you did," said Archer. "And didn't you miss seeing them?"

"Well, you've actually spent more time in Helmsley House than I ever did. I was only here—and only saw them—on summer breaks and holidays. They sent me to boarding school."

"They wouldn't do that," said Archer.

"They did," his father replied. "They were traveling much more back then and I was too young. They thought I would be better off at boarding school. And it was for the best."

"How could it have been?" said Archer. "What about all your museum stories? You never did what you wanted to do."

"That's not true," his father replied. "I loved hearing about my parents' adventures, but going on one myself? That's never been my interest. The museum was your grandfather's idea. After he met you, he made me promise to start taking you to the museum and tell you stories, which I was glad to do. But the stories I told were never my own. And they were never any good, were they?"

"They weren't terrible," said Archer.

Mr. Helmsley grinned and pointed a finger in the air.

"'World's greatest explorer!' That's pretty terrible. Your grandfather must have known they would be pathetic at best. I assume that's why they started sending you those boxes, but he must have *forgotten* to mention he'd be doing that. I take great pride in being their son, Archer, but I also take great pride in being the *only* boy in the history of the world who disappointed his parents by becoming a lawyer. I'm certain that's another reason your grandfather wanted you in Helmsley House. Just think how embarrassing it would be if both his son *and* grandson became lawyers?"

Archer's smile quickly faded. "And now I have to leave?" he said.

"I'm afraid so," his father replied. "But try not to look so miserable about it. A little country air can do wonders. You've been cooped up in this house for far too long. And besides, despite my best arguments in your favor, the Willow Academy hasn't decided whether to allow you back just yet."

Mr. Helmsley stood up, trying not to laugh.

"I can't quite figure it out," he said. "But something

about this whole tiger incident isn't sitting well with them. . . . And while it never should have happened in the first place, between you and me, I thought you handled that very well."

"Thanks," said Archer.

His father was about to leave the room, but Archer had one final question.

"Do you think they're still alive?"

Mr. Helmsley was silent a few moments, and when he spoke, he kept his back turned. "They had a good sense of humor about such things and so must we. But what I think doesn't matter, Archer. If you believe they are, it's important you go on believing so."

• A Little Peace •

Archer, Oliver, and Adélaïde spent their remaining days together on the rooftop. Across the gardens, the Murkley house was emptied and put up for sale.

"I still can't believe it was another polar bear," said Oliver. "Maybe you'll find out what happened at Raven Wood."

"Write to us if you do," said Adélaïde. "Well, write to us regardless."

Oliver leaned back on the roof. "I wish we had made it to the port," he said.

Both Archer and Adélaïde turned to him in surprise.

"It's not that I wanted to go," he clarified. "But I guess a part of me was looking forward to something new."

"A big part?" asked Adélaïde.

"No," said Oliver. "A very small part."

"Maybe it was just something you ate?" said Archer.

Adélaïde started giggling and she couldn't stop.

"It wasn't that funny," said Oliver.

"No, it's not that," she giggled. "I just keep wondering what those tigers must have thought when they spotted you in that gazelle mask."

When Adélaïde stopped giggling, she turned to Archer and said, "Miss Whitewood came to check on me yesterday. She wanted to come and see you, too, but wasn't sure if she should. She asked me to tell you she's sorry you're leaving and hopes she'll see you soon."

The Glubs were equally sorry to see Archer leave. Mrs. Glub gave him a tin of pastries for the train. And Mr. Glub reminded him to, "Keep bouncing along—bouncing merrily along."

Archer hadn't spent much time thinking about Raven Wood, but on the morning of his departure, it was all he could do. It was an unusual situation. He had always wanted to venture far away from Helmsley House. And now that he was, he didn't want to.

He rolled out of bed and went to the bathroom to wash his face and brush his teeth. Afterward, he went downstairs, hoping the newspaper would have another story about the museum fiasco. That would keep his mind busy. They weren't fully aware of it, but Archer, Oliver, and Adélaïde were quite famous due to the many stories written about them.

Archer opened the front door and bent down to pick up the paper, but quickly dropped it and turned his head. He blinked twice and then once more. He wasn't seeing things.

It's Adélaïde and Oliver's doing, he thought.

Leaning against the corner of the stoop was a green package tied with yellow string. And if it wasn't from Adélaïde and Oliver, the deliveryman was likely in a rush and had dropped it in a puddle because the box was soaked through. He inspected the soggy parcel. There was an address on it, but the ink had gone runny with the water. Still, he could just make out the name *Archer B. Helmsley*. He shut the door and returned to his room with the box.

✦

Next door, Oliver went barreling up the stairs with a copy of *The Doldrums Press* dangling from his fingers. Adélaïde was right behind him. At the same moment, reporters were once again swooping in from all directions to that tall, skinny house on crooked, narrow Willow Street. They held cameras and notepads and shouted questions at Mr. and Mrs. Helmsley, who were now standing in the doorway.

Oliver and Adélaïde nearly fell on their faces as they stumbled through Archer's balcony door.

"You saw it, didn't you!" cried Oliver, regaining his balance and holding up the newspaper. "The headline!"

THE DOLDRUMS PRESS

EXPLORERS DISCOVERED

"You should go look over the roof," said Adélaïde. "It's crazy down there. Oliver saw a reporter fall out of a tree!"

"He landed on three more when he fell!" said Oliver. "This means you won't have to go to Raven Wood!"

Archer knew this wouldn't change that. If anything, it would give his mother more of a reason to ship him off. But he was smiling from ear to ear. Oliver and Adélaïde sat down next to him on the bed. Oliver paled when he saw a chunk of ice in Archer's hands.

"We're not doing that again, are we?" he asked.

Archer handed him the note. Adélaïde read over Oliver's shoulder.

OCTOBER 19TH

ARCHER B. HELMSLEY
375 WILLOW ST.

ARCHER,

SORRY FOR THE SHORT MESSAGE. WE DON'T HAVE MUCH TIME. AND IT'S A LONG STORY. BUT WE KEPT A LITTLE PIECE OF THE ICEBERG. HOPE IT FINDS YOU BEFORE IT MELTS. SHOULD BE HOME BY CHRISTMAS. HAVE LOTS OF CATCHING UP TO DO.

YOURS TRULY,
Ralph and Rachel Helmsley

P.S. WE'VE BEEN OVERHEARING ODD REPORTS ABOUT A TIGER CHASE SOMEWHERE IN ROSEWOOD. THREE CHILDREN WERE INVOLVED. LUCKY TO BE ALIVE. WE'RE AMAZED. DO YOU KNOW ANYTHING ABOUT THIS?

Archer, Oliver, and Adélaïde sat quietly staring at one another.

"Do you think they dug?" Oliver asked.

Archer didn't know. He lifted the ice. "It's an iceberg," he said, and then lowered it a little. "Or at least, it's a piece of one."

"That's impossible," said Oliver.

"It should have melted by now," agreed Adélaïde.

They were both right. The ice should have melted long before it reached Archer. But it didn't. And what should have been didn't change the fact that Archer was now sitting on his bed, sharing a laugh with Oliver and Adélaïde while holding a piece of the iceberg. Or as Oliver put it, holding a piece of the impossible.